FULL HOUSE

SUSAN HAYES

CONTENTS

Opportunity doesn't always knock. Sometimes, it crash lands.

A veteran of the Resource Wars, Raze is a cyborg with a simple plan. He wants to be left alone, forever.

Planetary scout Sevda Rem is lightyears from civilization when her ship is damaged, forcing an emergency landing on an unoccupied planet. At least, it was supposed to be unoccupied...

He's trespassing on a corporate-owned planet. She's duty bound to report him. The deck is stacked against them, but if they play their cards right, they might discover that together they hold a winning hand.

Copyright © 2018 Susan Hayes

Full House (The Drift Series)

First E-book Publication: March 2018

Cover Design: Melody Simmons ~ ebookindiecovers.com

Editor: Dayna Hart

Published by: Black Scroll Publications

ISBN: 978-1-988446-26-4

For my parents for supporting my dreams even when they don't understand what drives me.
For my tribe, the ones who have my back and are always there with support, advice, and occasional a kick in the ass.
For my readers, because they are amazing. Thank you for reading my stories and joining me on this mad, wonderful adventure.

1
———

RAZE FELT the change in the weather coming before he even looked up. The breeze died, and the valley went quiet as the animals braced for what they knew was coming. The late spring weather was mild and pleasant most of the time, but not today. One of the first lessons he'd learned about his adopted home-world: when the valley went quiet, it was time to take cover.

The ax slammed down on the last of the wood, neatly splitting it. Only then did he straighten, rolling his shoulders as he looked up at the sky. It was still a cloudless stretch of deep blue, but he knew that wouldn't last long. Somewhere beyond the valley, a grandmother of a storm was brewing, and when it crossed the mountains, it would bring a deluge of rain and howling winds.

He gathered up the wood and carried it to the shed, stacking it with the rest of the morning's work. By the time he'd hung up the ax and secured the shed against the coming storm, the air was growing oppressive, and he was feeling restless. Storms always made him edgy. The wind and rain didn't bother him, but the crashing thunder and flashes of lightning that usually accompanied them reminded him of the past. Ten years of combat had left him with scars that would never heal and memories he couldn't let go.

From beyond the barn, a chorus of bleating started up. Apparently, he wasn't the only one feeling restless. "I'm coming. I'm coming. You'll be undercover long before the storm arrives, you woolly-faced fools."

The small herd of grazers he'd domesticated were all pressed up against the gate when he reached it, but it wasn't the storm that had them spooked. A new slash of white stood out against the blue sky. A contrail. He hadn't seen one of those since he'd been here, which was the whole point of moving to an unoccupied planet. He didn't want company.

A glint of silver caught his attention. There was definitely a ship up there, and judging by the angle of the contrail and its current altitude, it was coming in for a landing in his valley. *Fraxxing* wonderful. He kept watch until he was certain, his mood as stormy as the thunderheads that crested the mountains and darkened the sky as the unwanted vessel made an unsteady descent. By the time it touched down in the center of a clearing, near the river, it was clear that either the pilot was intoxicated, or the ship was badly damaged. Either way, they were in for an unpleasant afternoon. They'd parked on the valley's floodplain. Once the storm hit, it would send a torrent of rainwater pouring down the mountainsides in a deluge. Flooding was the reason he lived part way up the mountainside instead of down on the valley floor.

"I hope they can swim," he muttered before turning his attention to the animals pressing against the gate. Now that the strange thing in the sky was gone, they were calmer, but that wouldn't last long. He'd worry about the newcomer once he made sure his livestock were secured inside the barn.

The moment the gate opened the entire herd tried to push through at once, swarming around his legs in a woolly, bleating wave as they made straight for the barn. Not one of them wanted to be left behind, which was a clear warning that the storm was almost here. They had been wild animals only a few years ago, but now they were domesticated enough to want to stay out of the rain and weather.

He followed the animals at a more sedate pace, and by the time he got to the barn doors, they were settling in. The chickens were already roosting, and it only took him a few minutes to double check their feed and water supplies before closing them in for the duration of the storm.

With all the animals secured, he did a quick walk around the homestead to ensure that the greenhouses, outbuildings, and equipment were all secure and battened down. He was only feet from the front door of his home when the rain started to fall in thick, heavy drops. A gust of wind sent the rain flying sideways, and he broke into a jog.

He should have gone straight inside, closed the door, and stayed there until the storm ended, but something made him hesitate.

"They're not your problem," he reminded himself, but that didn't stop him from turning around. He could see the whole valley from his plateau, which was one of the reasons he'd picked this spot to build. With the small cliff behind him and a clear view of anything coming up the mountain, it was a safe, easily-defended location. Not that he had to defend it from much. The occasional carnivore came by to investigate his livestock, but that was it. It was a place of peaceful solitude, until today.

Movement down in the clearing confirmed he wasn't alone any longer. Even his cybernetically enhanced eyesight wasn't enough to pick out how many might be down there, so he reached inside the door and snagged his binoculars from the shelf. He trained the lens on the ship first. The black and green insignia on the side marked the ship as part of the Torex Mining corporation's fleet. Probably sniffing around to see if there was anything in the ground worth tearing apart the planet for.

The ship had to be a scout class. It was too small to be anything else. Minimal weaponry, sleek design, large engines and not much else. It was built for speed, not war. He moved on to the crewman currently examining the outside of the craft. It was getting hard to see through the heavy rain, but he could make out a few details. It was a female, humanoid, and quite tall. She had short, black hair and a curvy figure that not even her shapeless jacket could hide completely. Those curves affected him in a way that reminded Raze he hadn't been with a woman in years. It was a streak he had every intention of continuing. He wasn't fit company for anyone, and he never would be.

His hand brushed over the scars that marked the left side of his face and added streaks of pure white to his hair. He'd gotten them right here in this valley, in a battle that had cost him everything. The landscape had healed since then. Time and the elements had erased the damage or covered it over with greenery, but in his memory, he could see it all the way it had been. Broken, bloodstained, and raw.

A gust of wind howled past the cabin with enough force to make the walls tremble, and the already pounding rain increased until he couldn't see the ship or the woman any longer. If she didn't get back inside her ship soon, she was going to be in trouble. He set the binoculars back on their shelf, started to close the door, and stopped. It didn't feel right to leave her out there, on her own and unaware of what was headed her way.

He grunted in frustration at the sudden return of his conscience. He hadn't even been sure he had one anymore, but there it was, nagging at him to go out into the rain and make sure his unwelcome visitor didn't get herself killed. As he tugged on his rain gear, he tried to tell himself it was purely logical. If the Torex scout died, they'd send more ships to find out what happened to her. It was easier to save one and send her on her way than deal with the half dozen that would come looking later.

He was still trying to convince himself when he set out into the storm with a pack full of gear. He was buffeted by winds and hammered by the constant deluge of rain pouring out of the bruise-black clouds. He was drenched before he'd gone twenty feet from the cabin.

Whoever was down there, she already owed him, and they hadn't even met yet.

SEVDA WAS HAVING A LOUSY DAY, and it was getting worse by the second. The meteors that had struck her ship while she was in orbit might have been micro, but the damage they had done was huge. The hull was more or less intact, but one of the wings was shredded, and her ship's onboard computer still hadn't tracked down the cause of the power drains plaguing the ship.

It was amazing she had managed to maneuver the ship at all considering the damage she'd taken. Landing it safely had taken all her skill, and during the descent, she'd been thankful this planet was uninhabited. If she pancaked the ship on the surface at least there wouldn't be anyone around to witness her inglorious demise.

It would take Eddi and her team of maintenance bots several days to handle all the repairs if everything went smoothly. She looked around at the driving rain and already soggy ground. So far, things were not going smoothly at all.

She tapped the comm unit clipped to her jacket. "Eddi, run atmospheric scans and figure out how long this weather will last, will you?" The acronym of the ships AI was unpronounceable, so she had dubbed her Eddi after one of the workers on her parent's farm.

"Affirmative, Pilot Rem. Running now." There was a brief pause, then Eddi spoke again. "Initial assessment is that this weather will continue for at least several hours, possibly more. To get a better forecast, I would have to send one of my probes into the atmosphere. Current readings are limited by the mountains surrounding us."

"Don't waste your probes. They'll never make it to altitude. Not in this weather." She pulled up the hood of her jacket and sighed. This was supposed to have been nothing more than an orbital fly-by. Three days to scan the planet, send in her report, and move on. Landing hadn't been on the agenda, and every day they were here would make it tougher to collect her early-completion bonus. If she got that bonus, she'd have enough to pay off the last of her debts. She'd be free, but only if things didn't stop going wrong.

Frustrated and still feeling the aftereffects of her adrenaline-fueled descent, she decided to blow off some steam before returning inside. "Eddi, I'm going to do a quick recon before I come in. I'm already soaking wet, I might as well check out the area and stretch my legs while I'm out here. Have you started on repairs?"

"Maintenance bots have been deployed, and I am currently running diagnostics on all key systems. I would not suggest leaving the immediate area. My scans indicate a seventy percent chance of localized flooding in the near future, and the atmospheric disturbance caused by the storm may disrupt communications."

"You don't get to quote odds to me right now. You're the one who calculated that there was only a three percent chance of debris in our orbit and that it was safe to drop the shields to perform our scans." She pointed to the damaged section of the ship, aware that the computer program would be watching. "Does that look like three percent? From where I'm standing, it looks more like one hundred."

"As you have pointed out to me on numerous occasions, I am an imperfect program," Eddi retorted.

"I swear, you're getting to be more human every day. I'm not sure if that's a good thing or not," Sev muttered as she walked away from the ship and its quirky AI.

Despite her grumbling, it was nice to be outside of the ship. She was on a three-month assignment, which meant no time off and only a few brief returns to civilized space to stop at fully automated resupply stations.

This was the first time she had walked on a planet

in close to two months. The gravity was a little stronger than she was used to, but otherwise, it was a standard Goldilocks planet. Not too hot, not too cold, atmosphere and environment perfect for sustaining life.

She decided to go down to the river she had spotted during descent. It was only a brief walk, and if Eddi was right about potential flooding, she should probably check it out. If the water started rising, she might have to move the ship. "I'm headed to the river, Eddi. Let me know if anything changes here."

She found a narrow game trail and followed it, pausing now and then to unsnag her rain gear from a branch of the scrubby bushes and shrubs that lined the path. The wind was gusting hard enough to be a hindrance, too, and she was about to give up and turn back when the path finally widened and the bushes gave way to grass and open ground.

"Finally." She tapped her comms. "Eddi, can you read me? I'm down by the river, and I'm not seeing any signs of flooding here."

"Trans—cutting—recommend—retur—." Eddi's transmission was nothing but fragments followed by static.

Sevda tucked the comm device back under her jacket and snorted softly. "Well, she was right about the comms, but not the flooding. Imperfect program, indeed."

The river was only twenty feet away, the crystal-clear water tumbling over the rocks in a soothing rush that was almost musical. There had been a creek near the farm where she was raised, and that same sound had lulled her to sleep every evening until the night of the fire. After that, there was no more farm, no creek, no family, and no lullabies of any kind.

She closed her eyes and indulged herself in a rare moment of recollection. Sunny days and hard work, laughter around the kitchen table, the warmth of the livestock barn in winter. Colonizing a new world wasn't an easy life, but it had been a good one.

When she had enough money saved up to clear the last of her debts, it was a life she hoped to return to. She had worked most of her life toward making that dream a reality. Pushing herself from goal to goal until she could finally reclaim her life from Torex.

At first, the change in the river's song was too subtle for her to notice. It wasn't until the volume shifted from a steady rush to more of a roar that she became aware of it and opened her eyes. *Fraxx.* In the brief time she had been lost in thought, everything had changed. The formerly crystalline water was now muddy with silt and full of debris. Foliage and small branches sailed past, vanishing into the boiling cauldron of water. The outcroppings of rocks that had made such sweet music were covered now, and the water was rising with every passing second.

"Looks like she was right about the flooding, too. When I get back to the ship, I'm going to owe that pile of circuits an apology." Sevda turned and headed back the way she came. At least, she thought it was the right way. The bushes all looked the same through the driving rain, and the weather had already erased any trace of her footprints. She lowered her head against the wind and kept going. The wind had been pushing at her back on the way down, so if she walked directly into it, that had to mean she was going the right way.

She made it back to the scrub, but the river seemed to be following her. The water swirled around her boots, threatening her footing and slowing her even more. The increase in gravity that had seemed so minor before was far more evident now. It made slogging through the water even slower.

Panic reared its ugly head, and she tried her comms again. Nothing but static. Not that Eddi could do anything to help her, but it would have been nice to hear a friendly voice, even if it was a computer's.

A bolt of lightning arced across the sky, followed by a crack of thunder so loud she actually felt the shockwave roll through her. She stumbled, her foot caught on something beneath the muddy surface, and the next thing she knew she was face down in the water. Unseen rocks bit into her flesh and she yelped, sucking in a lungful of water. Her body convulsed into a fit of coughing to clear her lungs, and it was all she could do to get her face above the surface. Bruised, cold, and struggling to take a proper breath, she was carried away by the rising flood before she knew what was happening.

Everything seemed to happen in slow motion after that. Sevda could see what was coming, but there was nothing she could do to stop it. Every rock she hit, every wave that knocked her down into the cold, dark water, she got to experience it all in agonizing detail.

The cold water sapped her strength quickly, until even the slightest movement was a battle. All her life she'd been stronger than everyone else; one of the advantages of her mixed-species heritage. Being weak wasn't something she was used to.

Sevda was struggling to keep her head above water by the time she spotted the outcropping of rock rising ahead of her. It was her last chance. If she didn't catch hold of it, the river would win, and she'd die here on this nameless, starsforsaken planet with not so much as a grave to mark her final resting place.

The cold had made her weak and slow, but fortunately for her, there was one part of her that wasn't affected. She fought to get herself into the best possible position, and as she was swept past the rocks, she latched onto it with her right hand. The cybernetic limb responded, gripping the slick surface with inhuman strength. It wouldn't release as long as she remained conscious. Now, it was a matter of willpower. If she could withstand the flood, the cold, and exhaustion, she'd live. All her life, people had accused her of being too stubborn. It was time to find out if they were right. She gritted her chattering teeth and hung on.

2

———

RAZE MADE it to the valley floor just as the first bolts of lightning seared the sky. He eyed the trees around him and questioned his sanity for the hundredth time since leaving the cabin. The odds were good that his unwelcome visitor was safe in her ship, riding out the storm in total comfort while he traipsed around the woods, soaked to the skin and risking electrocution.

Being down in this valley with a storm in full force triggered a flood of memories he didn't want to revisit. Every crack of thunder ratcheted his tension up another notch, and he started falling into old habits, scanning the woods for enemies that didn't exist.

He stubbornly pushed on, as much to defy the ghosts of the past as to check on the ship's crew. He made it to the swollen edge of the river and followed it across the valley floor. He kept an eye on the flood waters, just in case he was wrong, and his visitor was foolish enough to be out in this storm.

He'd acquired several grazers in floods just like this one, fishing them out of the water and carrying them home to add to his herd. It wasn't a grazer he spotted this time, though. It was a flash of red that caught his eye. It vanished almost immediately, but he was watching now, and when the flash appeared again he got a better look—and started running. He wasn't the only one outside in this miserable storm, after all.

There were still thirty feet between him and the woman when she latched onto the rock with one hand. He expected her to last about two seconds. No human could have held on against the force of the current, but somehow, she did. The rock she was holding onto was only a few feet from the start of shallower water, but she had no way to reach it.

Options for getting out to her were limited, but he couldn't leave her there to die. "That's two she owes me," he said as he unslung the pack and started pulling out what he'd need.

"Can you hear me?" he shouted to her. He wasn't surprised when she didn't react. The water was likely deafeningly loud where she was, and the rock was between them, blocking her view.

He made preparations quickly, fastening one end of the rope to a tree, then putting on his safety harness and clipping himself to the rope. A few test pulls to ensure the knots held, and he waded into the water, bracing himself against the violent current by keeping a tight hold of the rope and letting it play out slowly.

He considered calling out again, but if he startled her and she lost her grip, he'd only have a second to catch her before she was swept away. Whatever strength she was using to keep hold of the rocks, he doubted she had enough left to save herself a second time.

When the rope was taut, and he was in position a few feet behind her, Raze braced his legs against the river bottom and made his presence known. "You picked a lousy day to go swimming," he said in Galactic Standard. It was the one language nearly everyone in the galaxy knew at least a few words of.

Her head whipped around and Raze found himself staring into a pair of dark brown eyes. To his surprise, her sudden movement didn't cause her to lose her grip.

"How? Where the *fraxx* did y-you come fr-rom?" she answered in the same language, though her words were broken by her chattering teeth.

He grinned. This one had nerves of steel, and a grip to match. "I live here. Do you really want to have this conversation here and now? I'm not up to my ass in cold water for my health here, sweetling. Let go of the rock, and I'll get you to shore."

"You b-better catch me, or I'm going to come b-back and haunt you as a very p-pissed-off ghost," she warned, her gaze locked on his.

"I've got you," he promised and opened his arms.

She nodded once and let go without another word. It was a demonstration of trust that hit him hard. No one had looked at him like that since... He cut off that line of thinking and focused on keeping his feet as she slammed into him with the full force of the river behind her.

There was an awkward tangle of limbs as they grappled with each other, but then she managed to wrap her legs around his waist, locking them together.

It was the first contact he'd had with another living soul in almost five years. The part of his heart he thought had gone cold and dark forever flared back to life, and so did his cock, which was a minor miracle considering the temperature of the water he was standing in. *That's not going to happen,* he reminded himself as he reached around her to grab hold of the rope and start pulling them both back to shore as fast as he could. Standing in the middle of a river during a thunderstorm wasn't the stupidest thing he had ever done, but it was in the top three.

Despite their circumstances, he couldn't help admiring the woman in his arms. She had to be close to six feet tall, and she held onto him with a strength some men couldn't have matched. She had guts, too. Letting go of that rock and trusting him to save her couldn't have been easy. She stayed silent and still, letting him concentrate on getting them to safety. If it wasn't for the fact he could feel her heart pound where they were pressed together, he wouldn't be able to tell she was anxious at all.

The second they were on dry land she released her legs from around his hips and let go of him, but her legs weren't steady enough for her to stay on her feet. He caught her as she started to drop, scooping her into his arms and carrying her to the tree where he'd left his things.

"You can p-put me down any t-time now," she said, shoving at his chest in mild annoyance.

"I will in a second. You've got to be tired and sore, not to mention cold. I'm *fraxxing* cold, and I was only in the water a few minutes." He paused. "And you're welcome, by the way."

She blushed slightly, bringing a faint touch of color to her cheeks. "S-sorry. Thanks for saving my life. Now, can you please p-put me down?"

"Sure thing, scout." He knelt down and set her carefully on the ground at the base of the tree. "You got a name?"

"Sevda. Sevda Rem, Scout, F-first class, Torex Mining Corporation exploration fleet. Nice to meet you—strange m-man who just happens to b-be wandering around an uninhabited planet. Please, if you're a smuggler, criminal, or lunatic, I'd rather n-not know your name, that way I won't have anything to put on my report."

He chuckled and shook his head. "None of the above. Name's Raze. I have a place on the eastern slope. You're the first person I've seen since I got here. What's a scout ship doing on the ground? You can't scan much from down here."

She shivered and wrapped her arms around herself

in an attempt to stay warm. Judging by the faint tint of blue in her lips and the way her teeth where chattering, she didn't have much body heat left to conserve. She needed to get somewhere warm and dry. Her ship would be best. She could dry off and be headed back to wherever she came from the moment the storm ended

He handed her the blanket, and she accepted it with a grateful smile that made his breath catch. Even soaking wet, covered in mud, and with a fresh bruise blooming on her cheek, she was damned attractive.

Annoyed with himself for even noticing, he made himself get to his feet and put some much-needed distance between them.

"You okay to walk? Your ship is about a ten-minute walk from here, and we should probably get going. You're not going to get any drier sitting out here in the rain, and with your luck, this tree will get hit by lightning any second."

She wrapped the blanket around her shoulders and nodded. "I'm ready when you are. *Veth*. Hang on a s-second, let me try and contact Eddi."

"Your crewmate let you go outside, alone, in this?" he demanded, waving at the storm overhead.

"Eddi's my ship's AI, and despite her attempts to nag me into doing what I'm told, I don't need her to *let* me do anything." Sevda pulled out a comm device and shook most of the water off of it. "Good thing these devices are waterproof. Eddi, do you read me?"

"You have been out of contact for some time, Pilot

Rem. I have been monitoring your position and status as best I could. You are some distance from my location and appear to be with another person. Are you in danger? Should I send a distress signal?"

"Stand down, Eddi, I'm fine. I got caught in the flood waters and a local fished me out."

"I did warn you that a flood was highly probable."

Raze didn't bother to hide his amusement and allowed himself a chuckle. Sevda was right, her ship's AI was a nag.

Sevda shot him an irritated look before continuing her conversation. "I'm returning to your position now. How are repairs going? And for that matter, why are comms working so well, now?"

"Repairs are underway. When your signal began moving rapidly, I reconfigured communications and increased power to boost the signal in case you needed to call for assistance. As for returning here, I do not recommend that course of action. I am currently surrounded by flood waters. Depth, three feet and rising."

"Tell Eddi you'll be staying with me until the storm ends and the water recedes."

What the hell was wrong with him? He didn't want this corporate scout on his planet, never mind in his home, disrupting his life. It was a bad idea, and he would know, he'd had his fair share of them.

Sevda blinked at him in surprise. "Stay with you?"

Apparently, she didn't think it was a good idea

either, which pissed him off even more than his own stupidity. What was wrong with coming home with him? He had saved her life, after all. It's not like he was more dangerous than the storm. "You've got three choices. Swim back to your ship, stay out here, or come with me." He gathered up his things and stuffed them into his pack. "What's it going to be?"

She shrugged and spoke into her comms. "Eddi, I'm going with Raze. The local resident I told you about. He's offered me shelter. Please monitor my location and initiate Sunrise Protocols."

He recognized the military code for 'monitor the situation and request back up as needed,' and chuckled again. "You're not going to need your ship to call for help, Sevda. You have my word, you'll be perfectly safe. If you vanish, Torex is going to come looking for you, and I have no interest dealing with them, or any corporation, ever again."

"You were military? How did an IAF soldier wind up way the hell out here?" She gestured around them at the empty planet.

"I wasn't with the Interstellar Armed Forces, but I do know the lingo. I'm out here because I like solitude."

"If you want to keep your solitude and avoid the corporations, you're going to have to pick a new planet to call home. This whole system is being assessed for future processing. I may be the first one here, but I won't be the last."

This day just kept getting better. He'd already

guessed as much, but suspecting something and having it confirmed weren't the same thing. He was going to lose everything, again. "You can tell me about Torex's grand plans for this place while we make the hike to my place. If I'm going to lose my home, it would be nice to know the details."

3

Sevda's brain was as scrambled and battered as her body. She was cold, bruised, and exhausted from her ordeal in the water. Now her only choice was to go with a giant of a man with a surly disposition to a cabin that shouldn't even be here, on a world that hadn't even been cursorily investigated yet.

Where the hell had he come from, and why was he way the *fraxx* out here? He'd pulled her out of the river, so she had at least one reason to trust him, but there were too many unknowns to be sure.

Then there was the other issue: he was hot as hell. A man that grumpy shouldn't be sexy, but he was. He had a full beard, but it didn't completely hide the fact he had several small scars on his face. There was a streak of white in his hair, but instead of detracting from his looks, it gave him character, and an air of danger.

His skin was deeply tanned, and his sun-streaked brown hair fell halfway down his back. There were callouses on his hands, too. She'd felt them snag on her clothes when he'd held her, and again when he passed her the blanket. This was a man who spent a lot of time working outdoors and had the body to prove it. She had been wrapped around him only a few minutes ago, and he was solid muscle and strength. Exactly the kind of man that made her weak in the knees - and in the head, apparently. The last thing she should be thinking right now was what he looked like under the heavy leather rain gear he was wearing, or what those calloused hands would feel like on her bare skin.

"I must have hit my head on one of those blasted rocks," she muttered to herself as she got to her feet. She was still half-frozen and bone-tired, but her legs were steadier and her teeth had stopped chattering. She was good to go.

"What was that?" Raze asked glancing over his shoulder.

"Nothing." She looked up at the sky and noted with some relief that the thunder and lightning seemed to have stopped while they were talking. "Looks like the storm is weakening."

He barked with laughter. "Not even close. That was the opening salvo. If we're lucky, we'll be undercover before the next one hits. If not, well, we can't get much wetter than we already are."

He set a brisk pace, and she had to scramble to catch up. She could have asked him to slow down, but she had a little pride left, and it wouldn't let her ask for any more favors. She owed him too much already. Besides, the sooner they got out of this weather, the happier she'd be. The wind was an icy knife that cut right through her, stealing what little body heat she had left.

They walked in silence for a while, but then he surprised her with a question. "How long do I have before I need to move on?"

She had been focusing all her energy on putting one foot in front of the other, and it surprised her how difficult it was to hold a conversation at the same time. "Hard to say. I was only supposed to do scans from polar orbit and move on to the next planet. I send the data as I finish each scan, and someone back at HQ reviews it all and figures out which planets are worth mining for resources. Usually, it takes about two years from first scans to a final decision, but that can change if the planet has exceptional value."

"And does it? This one, I mean. You've seen the scans, right? And what are you doing down here if you were supposed to stay in orbit?"

"I saw the first three hours of data. Then my ship was shredded by a micro-meteor swarm and I had to land to make emergency repairs."

"You really have had a lousy day, haven't you?"

She snorted with bitter laughter. "You could say that, yeah." As if to emphasize the point, she stumbled over a rock and went down in a tangled, sodden heap.

"*Fraxx*." Sevda tried to stand, but her body didn't

seem to want to cooperate. Suddenly all she wanted to do was curl up and nap for a little while. A little rest and then she could start walking again.

"That's it. You're done." For the second time that day she found herself in Raze's arms, and this time she was too tired to muster any kind of protest. To be honest, she was damned impressed he could lift her at all. Most men couldn't have done it. She was starting to suspect there was more to her rescuer's physique than just a lot of time spent outdoors.

"You sure you want to touch me? All this bad luck might be contagious." Her words came out a little slurred, and she frowned in frustration. What was wrong with her? Maybe she *had* hit her head on a rock during her involuntary swim.

He looked down at her with an odd half-smile. "I'll take my chances. You're in no shape to make the rest of the hike before the next storm hits." He settled her into his arms and started walking along the narrow trail that seemed to lead straight up the mountain.

One look at the trek they had to make, and she knew he was right. She didn't have the strength for that kind of climb. "You live way the hell up there? You really must not want visitors. "

"I don't."

"Don't you get lonely?" She gestured to her bruised cheek, then frowned when she noticed that her hand was still shaking. "What happens if you were seriously hurt? Don't you have a family or friends who worry about you?"

"If I got seriously hurt? I'd heal, or I'd die." He shrugged slightly, using the movement to shift her in his arms, so she was snuggled in tight to his body.

It was both distracting and comforting to be in such close contact with him, and because of that, it took her a moment to notice that he hadn't answered her second question.

"So, you're indifferent to your survival. No family then?" She had guessed the answer already. People with families didn't choose this kind of life.

"Nope."

She waited to see if he was going to say anything else, but apparently, that was all she was getting. Instead of trying to continue the conversation, she shut her eyes and tried to rest. There was no way he could carry her the whole way, and she was going to need all the energy she could muster once she was back on her feet.

At least she'd stopped shivering. That had to mean she was getting warmer, even if she didn't feel like it. She would rest up for another minute, no more. She wasn't some delicate flower that needed a hero to sweep in and carry her to safety.

AT FIRST, Raze was happy to make the hike in silence. He'd never been much for talking, and he had already spoken more today than he usually said in a month. It wasn't long, though, before memories started to stir;

recollections of the last time he'd carried someone out of this valley. In a few minutes, he would be walking past the graves of his cybernetic batch siblings. They had all died here, on this starsforsaken planet, during the Resource Wars. Cyborg soldiers like him had fought, bled, and died in a series of corporate battles that spanned the galaxy and lasted a decade.

Raze and his siblings were some of the first cyborgs created, and they had been to hell and back more times than he cared to count. They had lost a few of their number along the way, but out of his twenty-five original siblings, all but five were buried here. He carried them here himself, digging their graves and laying them to rest, one by one. It took him three days, and when it was done, he swore that if he survived, he'd come back one day. Back to the only family he had.

The dark memories threatened to drag him down, and he fought to keep his focus on the present. There were no enemy forces hunting for him anymore. No wars to fight. No danger.

No, that wasn't true. There was danger. The scout in his arms represented a threat he had no idea how to fight. She was also his only source of intel.

"Tell me what you know about Torex's plans are for this system." When she didn't answer, he looked down and discovered his visitor was unconscious. *Fraxx.* There was no way she'd drifted off to sleep while being carried. Something was wrong.

"Hey, scout. Sevda. This is no time for a nap. Open your eyes for me." He gave her the lightest of shakes, but she didn't move. Not so much as an eyelid flutter. He didn't have much experience with normal human injuries. Cyborgs were built to be stronger, faster, and endure far harsher climates. *Climates. Shit.*

He took a good look at her face. Even soaking wet and with a few cuts and bruises marring her face, she was still beautiful. She had soft features, golden skin, and dark lashes that fanned her cheeks. But beyond her appearance, something else struck him. Her lips still had a bluish tint, and her skin tone was a little ashy. He had his arms full holding her, so he bowed his head and pressed his cheek to hers. There was no warmth in her face—her skin was as cold as the river he'd pulled her out of.

He thought back to the moment she stumbled. He should have seen it then, but he hadn't spent much time with humans, and he'd forgotten they simply couldn't endure the same trials he could.

She was hypothermic. He needed to get her inside, dried off and warmed up, fast.

"You stay with me, Sevda. I'm not carrying another damned corpse up this trail." He tightened his grip on her and broke into a run.

He made it to the cabin in minutes, despite the slick footing and mud on the path. He pushed himself so hard he was out of breath, which wasn't something that happened often. He sprinted the last few feet across the cleared land of his farm and got them both under the porch and out of the weather. The rain was still pouring down, but the next wave of the storm hadn't hit yet. A quick hip bump to open the door and they were inside the welcoming warmth of his home.

He kicked the door shut and jogged across the cabin toward the alcove he used as a bedroom, right beside the woodstove he used to heat the cabin. He placed her carefully on the bed and pulled all the blankets from the far side over her in a temporary cocoon. It wouldn't be enough, but it would stop her from getting any colder. At least, he hoped it would.

"I'll be right back," he told her, and moved a few feet away to strip off his wet gear and wring some of the water out of his hair. He was soaked to the skin, but unlike Sevda, the cold and wet didn't bother him. The nanotech in his blood did more than keep him in perfect health, it helped him regulate his body temperature no matter how extreme the weather was. He tossed his still-dripping clothes into a corner, pulled on a pair of loose-fitting pants and then grabbed an armload of wood from the wood box. Once the fire was stoked, he looked back at Sevda. She hadn't stirred at all.

Time for more drastic measures.

"You can slap me for this later, but right now, I need you out of those wet clothes," he said. It wasn't likely she would hear anything he said, but he had to say it anyway. If his siblings could see him now, they'd all be laughing their asses off. Raze, the silent, stoic one, reduced to a chatty nursemaid.

Once he had the blankets pulled back, part of the problem became obvious. He had been too busy to notice before, but Sevda's outfit was far too lightweight to provide any protection from the elements, and it wouldn't have been enough to hold in any of her body heat. It clung to her like a second skin beneath her thin rain jacket. All she was carrying was her comm device and a blaster, both of which he placed out of reach before returning to the task of getting her warm and dry.

He got her boots and jacket off easily enough, but the rest of her clothes resisted every attempt he made to gently remove them. With a grunt of frustration, he tugged open a drawer on the bedside table he'd made himself and pulled out one of the multi-purpose tools he'd brought with him. "Sorry, but I'm about to ruin your outfit, too. By the time you wake up, I'm going to have a list of things to apologize for."

He cut her out of her clothes as quickly as he could and tried his best to keep his gaze locked on his hands and not on the beauty lying in his bed. It wasn't easy. With every inch of her skin that he uncovered, his libido paced at its leash like a panther on the prowl. He was doing this to get her warm, not to get her naked. He would keep reminding himself of that until his cock finally got the message.

He finally got all but her underwear removed, and by then he knew that the fire and blankets wouldn't be enough. Her skin was chilled everywhere he touched her, and she still wasn't awake. He lifted her again, holding her limp body against his chest while awkwardly moving back the blankets enough he could get her beneath them.

Once she was settled on the bed, he pulled the covers over her and added the few spare blankets on top for good measure. Then he slid in beside her and pulled her into his arms so her back was to his chest. He tucked her head under his chin and wrapped his arms and legs around her, sharing his body heat.

"And here I never figured I'd have a woman in my bed again."

A little time later she stirred. "So c-cold."

"I know you are, sweetling. I'm doing what I can to fix that." It was a relief to hear her speak again. If she was awake, then the odds were good she would make a quick recovery.

She burrowed under the blankets, wriggling her mostly naked body against his until he was half out of his mind. "Lie still, Sevda. You need to rest."

"Tired," she muttered in what sounded like agreement.

"Then sleep. I've got you. You're safe."

She finally quieted, but the peace didn't last for long. As her body temperature rose, she started to shiver hard enough he had to tighten his grip on her to hold her still. Her teeth chattered so violently that her next attempt to talk was almost intelligible.

"Wh-wh-at iz wro-wrong wi m-me?"

"Hypothermia. You were in the water long enough your body temperature dropped, and you weren't dressed for the elements. I'm not used to humans, I forgot you'd be affected by the weather, too."

"Not, just hu-human. Torski, t-too."

Well, that explained a few things. Torksi's were larger than humans and far stronger. They also had a higher body temperature. "So that's why you're so tall. I wondered."

"Hot-t-t blooded t-too." She managed to twist around in his arms so that she was on her back looking up at him.

Her eyes made sense to him now. He'd thought they were brown at first, but now he'd taken a better look, he realized there was a cluster of black around her iris. All or partially black irises were another Torski trait. Curious, he slipped a hand under the covers and took her hand in his, counting her fingers. Five. Well, she didn't have all the traits of her alien side, or there would only have been four.

She seemed to know what he was checking, because she bared her teeth, revealing her canines were elongated into prominent fangs. "Got-t the t-teeth, though."

The first thought that crossed his mind was to wonder how those sharp points would feel raking across his skin. He was still lost in thought when he realized she was watching him intently, waiting for his reaction with a guarded expression. He knew the look. He'd worn it often enough himself while he waited for people to turn away. Sometimes it was the scar on his face that did it, but most of the time, it was the moment they realized what he was: a cyborg. To most, that made him nothing more than a killing machine, a corporate-owned creation with a barcode on his wrist and no soul.

He offered her a confession of his own in exchange. Without a word, he held up his left wrist to show her the barcode imprinted on his skin. Instead of pulling away, she reached up and stroked her thumb across the mark.

"Th-that 'plains why you're s-so damned b-big. I wond-dered." She tossed his own words back at him with a hint of a smile.

He actually laughed at that. "You must be feeling better."

She nodded, her hand still on his arm. That was the moment she realized her own arm was bare. Her eyes narrowed, and then she started scrambling to put some distance between them, which put her in jeopardy of falling out of bed.

"Clothes!" She managed to get out the single word without her chattering teeth breaking it up.

"You're not wearing many. No. Now stop flailing before you end up on the floor with a concussion to add to your list of injuries." He lifted the blanket and pointed out the fact he was still wearing pants. "I'm still mostly dressed, but skin to skin contact was the only way to get you warmed up. I don't exactly have a med-bay in my cabin. Options were limited."

"That b-bad?"

He nodded. "You don't remember getting here, right?"

She shook her head.

"That's because you were out of it. I couldn't rouse you, and that worried me. I should have made sure you were warmer before we started walking back to the cabin, but I'm not used to worrying about anyone else, especially not a non-cyborg."

"Shirt?"

She must have decided that if she kept to single words, it was easier to talk.

"I can get you one of mine. Yours -- uh, I had to cut it off."

She arched a brow at that.

"Does it look like I get a lot of practice undressing beautiful women out here? I went with the expedient solution."

"Shirt. Please."

Something about the way she said it breathed life back into a part of his heart he thought had died the day he buried his siblings.

"I'll be right back. I don't promise it'll be fashionable, but it'll be clean." He got out of bed and went to fetch her a shirt, ignoring the part of his brain complaining that he much preferred her to stay naked.

That part of his brain needed to shut the hell up. Naked or swaddled in three layers of blankets, it wouldn't matter. Nothing was going to happen. Once she could get back to her ship, the sexy scout would fly out of his life. Maybe she'd repay him for saving her life by making sure that his planet stayed off Torex's radar. All he wanted was to be left alone.

It wasn't much to ask after all he'd been through. So, why the *fraxx* wasn't the universe cooperating?

4

———

Sevda woke with a start. What the hell was that noise? Had something hit the ship? "Eddi, report!" The words were out of her mouth before she was even fully awake.

"Welcome back to the land of the living," drawled a male voice that was most definitely not her ship's AI.

A name popped into her aching head. "Raze?"

"Mhmm."

She sat up and got her first look at her surroundings. This was not her ship, and Raze was...wow. No wonder she remembered him. He was big, sexy, gruff, and...not wearing much.

She ignored the screams of protest from her bruised and battered body and scrambled out of bed, then nearly jumped out of her skin when another boom of what had to be thunder shook the walls of the cabin.

"What happened? Where are we, and where the

fraxx are my clothes?" She was wearing her panties and a shirt two sizes too large for her, and as far as she could tell, that was it.

Raze chuckled and rose up on one elbow, baring more of his heavily muscled chest. "At least you're consistent. That's pretty much the first thing you asked me the last time you woke up."

"What was your answer the last time? And when was that?" She shook her head, trying to clear some of the cobwebs, but all that did was make her headache worse.

"You landed your ship in my valley, went for a walk during a thunderstorm, and got caught in a flash flood. I fished your soggy ass out, you checked in with Eddi, and then I carried you back here, to my home. Hypothermia's a bitch. I saved your life. You're welcome."

His grumpy delivery jogged her memory even better than his recital of the facts. She remembered him catching her in the cold floodwaters and his casual dismissal of what would happen to him if he got hurt out here on his own. He was like her, alone in the universe.

"Thank you." She rubbed her aching head and sat down on the edge of the bed.

"Again, you're welcome. How are you feeling?"

"Like I got bounced across a riverbed and nearly drowned in the process. I'm stiff and sore, but I'll live. I'd ask for a pain-blocker, but given what you are, I guess you don't have any need for them, do you?"

"Afraid I don't have anything like that." He frowned for a moment, then snapped his fingers. "But I do have something that should help. It's an ointment I use on the noats. At least, I try to use it. The stupid beasts like the taste so much they keep licking it off."

"What's a noat?"

Raze got out of bed before answering, revealing more of his stunning physique, and a body with more than a few scars. Cyborgs had been created to fight in what the corporations called bloodless wars, but judging by what she could see, he'd suffered and bled more than she could imagine.

"They're an indigenous herbivore. My batch brother, Slash, named them noats because they're not goats, but they're similar. Not goats – noats."

"You have a brother out here? I thought you didn't want company?"

His sea-blue eyes turned stormy. "I don't. I'm alone."

He walked away without another word. Perfect. She'd been awake for less than five minutes, and she had already managed to piss off the only other self-aware lifeform on the planet.

"This is why I work solo," she muttered to herself.

The floor was cold under her bare feet, so Sevda climbed back under the covers while she watched Raze check the contents of several drawers until he found what he was looking for.

"Try that." He lobbed the container to her.

"Thanks." She caught it automatically, then winced

as hot pokers of pain stabbed into her shoulder. Her cybernetic prosthetic merged with her body just above the elbow, which meant that her shoulder and upper arm had taken a lot of abuse while she had clung to the rock. Might as well start there.

She opened the container and the scent of camphor, mint, and a host of herbs she didn't know the name of, instantly transported back in time. Her mother had used this ointment, or something very like it, to fix everything from aches and bruises to sore throats and chest colds.

Amazed, Sevda lifted the container to her nose and breathed in deeply, not caring that the fumes were strong enough to bring tears to her eyes. She could almost hear her mother's voice and feel the gentle touch of her hand.

"It stinks, but it works," Raze said.

"I know this stuff. My mom called it her magical fix-anything medicine. I haven't seen it in years, though." She gently applied some of the ointment to her cheek. She didn't need a mirror to know she had a bruise there, she could feel it. After that, she scooped out a dollop with her fingers and smoothed it onto her bicep, belatedly realizing she should have rolled the sleeve up first.

"Magical fix anything medicine, huh?" Raze reappeared at the door of the sleeping alcove and crouched in front of the wood stove.

"Mhmm." Sevda was trying to focus on massaging the

goop into her aching muscles, but her gaze kept straying to the chiseled god crouched only a few feet away. If things were different, she'd be tempted to reach out and touch him right now. Hell, she was tempted to do it anyway, and that was probably the worst idea she'd had today. He had made it clear he liked his solitude, and while he'd been kind enough to save her life, that didn't mean he'd welcome a sexual overture from a mixed-race mutt like her. Not to mention the fact that her arrival meant his time on this planet was likely coming to an end.

When he opened the door of the stove, she stopped breathing. Flames licked at the logs as he tossed fresh wood on the fire. Fire. She hadn't seen a fire burning in years. She lived in a high-tech world of space travel and artificial atmospheres, where fire wasn't just archaic, it was *fraxxing* dangerous.

"You okay?"

She shook herself free of the memories and discovered Raze was standing in front of her, a look of concern softening his eyes and making him even more attractive. "I'm okay. It's just been a long time since I saw an open flame. Or smelled old-fashioned ointment, or sat in a log cabin while a storm raged outside for that matter. It's all taking me back to my childhood."

"You grew up like this?" Raze sounded utterly stunned by the idea.

"Well, our farmhouse was by a creek instead of halfway up a mountain, and we had cows and sheep, not noats, but yeah, otherwise this all feels sort of familiar."

Raze took the ointment out of her hand and sat down beside her on the bed. "Give me your arm. You're going to tie yourself in knots trying to apply it to yourself."

She lifted her right arm and he drew it toward him, holding her wrist gently as he started working the ointment into the aching muscles of her upper arm. It was hard to think of something intelligent to say when he was touching her, turning her brain gooey, so she didn't say anything at all.

He broke the silence stretching between them. "How did you end up working as a scout pilot? You're a long way from home, aren't you?"

She snorted. "We're both a long way from *everything*."

"True. But it doesn't answer my question." His chuckled, working his way down her arm.

"I was orphaned when I was thirteen. I had no other family, so I ended up in a corporate-run facility." It was a simple summary of what had been a nightmarish time in her life. Alone and grieving, she had been little more than a shadow of her former self; barely speaking, rarely sleeping, and fed a scant diet of food-tabs and nutri-gruel.

"That sounds unpleasant. Having been a guest of the corporations, I have firsthand experience of their idea of hospitality."

"It wasn't as bad as what you lived through. They

couldn't get much work out of us if they didn't keep us healthy."

"If you disliked being under corporate control, why did you stay?" he asked without looking up from what he was doing.

"I didn't have a choice. We were billed for room and board, clothes, even our education." She pointed to a thin scar that circled her arm above her elbow. "I lost an arm in the fire that killed my family. It was crushed and burned so badly they had to amputate. I had a basic prosthetic, but the only way to get something better was to sign on with the corporations and have them pay for it."

His calloused fingers traced the scar with fascination. "I would never have guessed. It looks well... real." He winced. "And now I sound like one of the idiots who would make those same comments to me. I'm sorry."

"Coming from you, it doesn't have the same negativity attached. Hell, I should probably be thanking you. My arm works so well because it's based on the same tech as yours."

Raze ran his hand down her arm until he could close his fingers around hers. "I'm starting to realize we have a lot in common. We both like solitude. We're both outsiders. We share the same technology."

"And we've both lived under the thumb of the corporations. The only difference is, you escaped. I haven't. Not yet."

"Not yet? So one day you'll be free?"

She nodded, and her heart tripped a little faster in her chest. Soon. Soon, she'd make her final payment and fly away to start a life somewhere. Her life would finally be her own. "I've spent the last fifteen years working for Torex. When I'm finished this last run, I should have enough scrip saved up to pay the last of my debts.

I'm almost free."

RAZE SAW the determination and hope gleaming in Sevda's eyes and understood exactly what she was feeling. There had been a time when he felt the same way. Those memories stirred feelings that he thought he had buried with his siblings. They hit him hard, filling the emptiness he'd lived with for years. He kept hold of her hand and pulled her in close enough to look into her eyes. He bowed his head and claimed her mouth with a hunger fuelled by years of loneliness. He knew he was overstepping every line there was. She had every right to slap him, or scream, or shove him away, but instead, she uttered a soft moan and kissed him back with a fervor that matched his own.

They ignited like a spark hitting a tank of rocket fuel. Hard kisses. Light touches. Hands tugging at clothing. Her lips parted with another moan, and he slipped his tongue into her mouth, eager to taste her. A hint of spice. Cinnamon? He didn't really care what it was, only that he wanted more.

He tore his mouth from hers to plant a line of open-mouthed kisses along her jaw and down the curve of her throat. She tipped her head to the side, offering herself to him, and he let himself get lost in the scent and taste of her body. Hard muscles under silken skin, that elusive whisper of cinnamon again, and her.

Her fingernails raked down his back, following his spine down to the waistband of his pants. She slid her fingers under the fabric and sank her nails into his flesh.

"More," she whispered, her voice gone rough with need.

"So much more. Everything. Just say yes."

Her hypnotically dark eyes widened and a smile curved her lush lips into a smile that promised a thousand pleasures. "Yes."

That was all the permission he needed. The storm outside was no match for the one raging inside him as he rose to his feet. "Shirt off."

She smirked at him. "Bossy."

"You have no idea. Now, get my shirt off before I decide not to lend you any more clothes for the rest of your stay."

She bared her fangs at him and stuck out her tongue for good measure, but she skinned the shirt over her head and let it drop to the floor without another word of argument. Her panties came off next, and when she straightened to look at him, he forgot to breathe.

She was beautiful. Strong. Curvy. Soft and sassy. He wouldn't have to worry about hurting her. She wasn't a delicate human woman. She was so much more.

She reached for him, and before he realized what she intended, his pants were torn apart and the tattered remains fluttered to the floor beside his shirt.

"Now you owe me a pair of pants."

Sevda laughed and wrapped her fingers around his cock, making it hard to think of anything except how good it felt to have her touching him.

"And you owe me a set of clothes. Shall we call it even?"

"Vixen."

"You have no idea." She pumped her fist over his steel-hard dick, then leaned down to swipe her tongue across the tip. He buried his fingers in her dark curls and cradled her head in his hands as she hummed in pleasure and took him deeper into her mouth.

His balls tightened, and his next breath came out in a strangled hiss. Nothing had ever felt this good.

She chuckled softly and released his cock to grin up at him. "Nothing, huh?"

Damn. Did I say that out loud? Judging by her grin, he must have.

"Nothing, ever," he clarified.

Her smile turned wicked. "Good."

She lowered her mouth to the crown of his cock again, and this time she dragged the delicate point of her fang across the tip before taking him deep. Her hand pumped his length as her hot little mouth devoured him. She worked him with her tongue, her teeth, and her fingers, teasing and tasting until his legs were unsteady and he was on the verge of losing the last shreds of his control.

"Enough. When I come the first time, I want to be inside your pussy, fucking you until you scream my name."

There was a gentle pop as she released his cock. Then she scooted back onto the bed with a welcoming smile that turned his insides to molten metal. This beautiful, sexy woman smiling that way at *him*. The scarred one. The broken machine.

"Maybe I want to hear you scream mine." She crooked a finger at him as another blast of rain and water slammed against the walls of the cabin.

"Let's see who screams first."

He was on top of her in a second, and she buried one hand in his hair, pulling him in for a kiss so hot it seared his soul. Her free hand rose up to touch his face, exploring his scars with her fingertips.

"These are sexy," she whispered.

"I'm damaged."

"So am I."

Damaged was the last word in the galaxy he'd use to describe the beauty staring up at him. Sexy. Intriguing. Beguiling. Those were the words he'd use. "I don't think so."

For a moment, he thought she was going to argue. Instead, she tugged on a lock of his hair until their lips were a breath apart. "Then shut up and kiss me."

Tongues dueled as their naked bodies rubbed against each other, setting him on fire all over again. He needed to touch her, to stroke and explore every inch of her body. Without warning, he rolled them over so that she was on top, and she laughed as she straddled him. Her slick pussy pressed against his dick, their bodies so close he could feel the pulse and flex of her inner walls before he was even inside.

"Much better." He reached up to cup her breasts, letting their warm weight fill his hands as her nipples pebbled beneath his palms.

"Mhmm." She leaned forward, leaning into his touch.

He tweaked a tender nipple with his fingers, aware they were still lightly coated with ointment. Her breath caught as the menthol and other ingredients made her skin tingle, and when he did it to her other nipple, she moaned and surged against his hand.

That simple movement rocked her hips against his cock, snapping a few more threads on his control. "Do that again and things are going to move faster than I planned."

She ground herself over him in a long, slow swing of her hips. "This?

"You were warned."

She wrapped her fingers around his wrists and laughed as he bucked his hips hard, and shifted positions so he was notched at her entrance. They held eye contact as he slid into the heat of her body. She was perfect. Hot and tight and already so wet he didn't stop until he was balls deep inside her. He groaned her name.

Sevda threw back her head and uttered a wild cry of pure need that resonated deep in his heart. This was what they both needed. The storm, the world, and the loneliness faded away. His cock twitched, then started to throb. A gentle thrust, a gasp, and she started to move with him.

She was liquid fire wrapped around him, riding him harder with each rise of his hips. With every breathless cry she made, he lost a little more control. Harder. Faster. Wilder. She let go of his arms to brace herself against the bed, her lips finding his. She screamed his name, the sound captured by his mouth. She gave herself over to him, a creature of pure pleasure. His. Hers. Theirs.

He kept one hand on her breast, the other cradling the back of her head as they flew together, two hawks riding the winds of a tempest until he finally reached the height of ecstasy. He came in silence, too far gone to summon any words, not even her name. She shuddered atop him, sitting up to reach between them and bringing herself over with a touch of her fingers.

It was the sexiest thing he'd ever witnessed.

She slumped onto his chest in a breathless heap, and he found himself wanting to stay like that. It was a dangerous temptation. She wasn't staying. He wasn't going anywhere. This was never going to be more than a brief respite for either of them.

A muffled comment drew him out of his dark thoughts and made him smile.

"You screamed my name first." She declared, lifting her head to flash him a triumphant, if flushed, grin.

"I don't recall it happening that way. I said your name. You screamed mine."

"And here I thought all cyborgs had perfect recall. Yours is clearly faulty."

"I'm in perfect working order." He grinned at her as an unfamiliar lightness filled him. "Or do you have complaints to file?"

"*Veth*, no. No complaints. If you worked any better, I'd probably die of satisfaction." She flexed her inner walls around him, and his cock twitched as a fresh surge of blood rushed south.

"You've already had one near-death experience today. If you don't want to risk another one, you might want to keep still."

"If I didn't like danger, I'd be in a different line of work." She made a show of looking around his cabin. "Besides, unless you've got a holo-vid player tucked away somewhere, there's nothing else to do until my ship is repaired and this storm ends."

"I don't have a lot of tech in here." His cabin was rustic, but that didn't mean he didn't have a vid player or most of the other modern conveniences. He just didn't use them. They were stashed onboard his ship; which was parked only a few yards away from his cabin. He housed it inside a building designed to shield it from the elements...and from being detected by passing ships like Sevda's.

"I noticed. You live simple." She touched the wall. "But snug. I like it."

Pride filled him. Raze had never expected anyone else to ever see what he'd built out here. It surprised him that her approval meant so much to him—but it did. "it's not much, but it's more than I ever had before. And you're welcome to stay here with me, in my snug cabin, for as long as it takes to get your ship fully repaired."

"Thank you." She stroked his cheek. "

5
_____

WHEN SEVDA CAME TO AGAIN, the cabin was empty. Judging by the full mug of still-warm coffee beside the bed, her rescuer-turned-lover hadn't been gone for long, though.

Raze had also left an assortment of clothing on the end of the bed. Coffee and a change of clothes, but no note. The man was definitely used to living alone. She rose from the bed and stretched out her bruised and aching body before trying on the garments. It was the first time in her life that everything she tried on was too big for her, but she eventually managed to find something that would at least keep her warm and covered.

She was dressed before it occurred to her that the storm had passed. The wind and rain were gone, at least for the moment. A quick check of the cabin showed her the location of the facilities, and she quietly thanked whatever higher beings were within earshot that Raze's simple lifestyle did not exclude running water and indoor plumbing. She had no idea how he'd managed it, and for the moment, she didn't care.

With coffee in hand, she did a more thorough exploration of the cabin and discovered that while Raze lived a simple existence, he hadn't eschewed all technology. There were electric lights, a small refrigeration unit, and a simple stove in the cabin. Most people would never understand living like this on purpose. She did, though. It wasn't an easy way to live, but it was what she wanted for herself. Even if it meant giving up the comforts of ship life and the company of stubborn AI's.

Veth. Eddi.

Her comm unit was on the dresser. "Eddi, status report."

"Soggy."

"Would you care to expand on that remark? Keep in mind I've had very little caffeine and nearly died yesterday."

"If you had listened to me, I did warn you that flooding was—"

"Eddi, what have I told you about backtalking?"

The AI changed topics without further comment. "My status is that I'm currently surrounded by floodwater. Peak depth never reached my fuselage, though I believe I took some minor structural damage to my landing struts. I will not be able to confirm until the water has fully receded. It should be safe for you to return in approximately thirty-six hours."

"Did you have any trouble withstanding the flood? Any significant damage to any system or structure? What's the repair timetable?"

"I deployed my stabilizers and grapplers when the water rose high enough to be a concern. I did not incur any significant damage. I am a Seeker Class vessel, not some thin-hulled shuttlecraft. It would take more than water and foliage to interfere with my operation."

She probably shouldn't pick a fight with her ship, but Sevda couldn't help herself. "Apparently all it takes is a micro-meteor swarm to put you out of commission. Or did you forget why we're on this backwater planet in the first place?"

Eddi remained silent for an extra two seconds, just long enough to convey her opinion of Sevda's remark. "The damage I incurred during the flood will not add more than a few hours to my overall repair time. I estimate I will be fully repaired in forty-eight to fifty hours. Will you be fully functional by then?"

"I'm fine, Eddi. Bruised and sore, but nothing worse than that. I will be staying with Raze until the floodwaters recede to safe levels. Once the skies are clear, I'd appreciate it if you sent a drone with a med-kit." The drones were for reconnaissance and scanning, but they could carry a small payload as well. An emergency med-kit would be about as much as one of them could manage, but it would do.

"Affirmative. I will deploy a drone to deliver the requested items shortly."

"Thank you. Oh, and be sure to include some pain-blockers. Raze doesn't have any."

She signed off and set the comm unit back on the side table. It would seem that for the next day or so, she was on unofficial shore leave.

It didn't take long for her to find a coat and boots she could borrow. Her boots were still drying by the woodstove, and she had learned the hard way that her light jacket was no match for the elements on this planet. The boots were too big, but if she took smaller steps, she could manage.

Raze wasn't in sight when she got outside, but there were plenty of things that caught her interest. The cabin was built on a plateau that appeared to span several acres before becoming steep hillside again. There were two greenhouses near the edge of the plateau, along with several other sheds and outbuildings, and a large, sturdy looking barn. One of the barn doors was open, and she decided to check and see if Raze was inside.

Walking helped to ease some of the stiffness from her muscles, but she knew better than to push herself.

As she neared the door, a chorus of bleating rose up from behind the fenced pen built onto the side of the barn. The noise distracted her from her planned destination, and she went to the fence instead.

"What have we got here? You must be the noats."

There were more than a dozen herbivores inside

the pen. They had cloven hooves, small horns, and their woolly coats were marked with piebald patches of white and brown. When they rushed the fence, she leaned over to pat them, and they greeted her like a long-lost friend instead of a stranger.

"You're adorable. Would you like some fresh grass? I bet you would. Hang on a second and I'll find you some."

Feeling like she was a kid back on the family farm, she went in search of something to feed her new, woolly friends.

***

RAZE ROSE EARLY, even though he hadn't slept much. The constant barrage of the storm had filled his dreams with memories of battles and bloodshed. More than once he'd imagined himself back on the path, carrying another dead body up the trail to the grave-yard he'd built for his family. Each time he woke, he'd find Sevda curled up in his arms, and the comforting warmth of her body had helped to calm him. He'd made love to her some of those times, and other times he'd simply held her until he drifted off to sleep again. Then the nightmares would return, and the cycle would start over.

He busied himself checking the pens and then releasing the animals from the barn and feeding them, then did a careful check of the greenhouses and other buildings to make sure they hadn't been damaged in the storm.

He had finished those tasks and was heading back to the cabin to check on his unexpected guest when he heard something he'd never heard before. Peals of female laughter.

He found her inside the noat pen, seated on a chunk of wood that he used to prop the gate open on windy days. She was surrounded by the woolly animals, chattering away and laughing as she fed them handfuls of fresh grass she pulled from the pockets of her borrowed coat.

In the years he'd been here, he had never imagined what it might be like to have someone to share the work with. Someone who actually enjoyed the kind of life he led.

"Your master takes good care of you, doesn't he? I bet he takes better care of you lot than he does himself. Of course, he doesn't need to worry about getting sick or injured, his medi-bots take care of all that."

She pulled out another handful of grass and laughed as they leaped over each other to try and get at it. "Don't be greedy! There's plenty where that came from."

A heavily pregnant female pushed her way through the milling throng, shoving her head into Sevda with enough force to knock her over. He was about to vault the fence to pull her out when her piping laughter filled the air.

"Manners, little lady. Just because you're eating for

two doesn't mean you can be so pushy." Sevda reappeared, covered in mud and grinning. She plonked herself back onto her makeshift seat and handed the noat that had knocked her over a generous handful of grass.

While the animal chewed on its snack, Sevda ran a hand along the noat's pregnant belly, pressing in at several spots, then repeated the entire process again on the noat's other side. "My mistake. You're not eating for two, you're eating for three."

"She is? How can you tell?" The question popped out before he remembered he hadn't announced his presence.

Sevda's head snapped around. "Raze! I swear, you need to wear a bell or something, so I know where you are."

"I'm not used to having anyone around to startle." He walked over to the fence and vaulted over the top railing, landing in a space clear of animals. "I see you've met my noats."

"I was making friends with them. They're very sweet."

He chuckled as the herd rushed in to butt their heads against his legs in greeting.

"You've fed them, they're your friends for life, now."

"You mean until I have to leave."

He didn't like being reminded she was leaving soon, and he didn't like that he didn't like it.

"You were going to show me how you know Seventeen was carrying twins."

"You named her Seventeen? What kind of name is that?"

"A practical one. She was the seventeenth noat to join the herd."

"We need to work on your imagination. I think she looks like a Lucy."

She expected him to laugh at her, but instead, he crouched down beside the beast and put a gentle hand on her head.

"Then that will be her name. So, how do you know she's carrying more than one baby?"

Sevda crouched beside him, guiding his hand over the noat's side and belly as she showed him what to feel for. When they reached the second twin's head, it moved, making their hands jump.

"Veth. I felt that. Was that its head? It felt like it." He was so excited it made her heart go gooey.

"That's its head, yep. Poor Lucy, there's not a lot of room in there for those two. I'd bet my next bonus she's going to be in labor in the next couple of days."

"How do you know so much about a species you've never seen before?"

She laughed. "I grew up on a farm, remember? We raised all kinds of livestock. Some of it to sell, others for food, or wool, or milk. I might not have seen a noat before, but I can make some educated guesses."

He gave her a thoughtful look. "You really want to go back to living like this? No more traveling the stars?"

"More than anything. I want dirt under my boots and fresh air to breathe. I was a pilot because that's what the aptitude tests said I was good at. I became a scout because it meant I had a chance to pay off my debts before I died of old age." She raised her hand from Lucy's side to point around them. "Someday, I'm going to have a place like this."

"it's a lot to take on. More than I ever thought there would be. It won't be easy." There had been times when he wished that he had someone to share the work, or at least keep him company through the long, lonely times when there wasn't enough work to distract him from the fact he was alone on the planet. The isolation was necessary, though. He had made a promise to his siblings, and he intended to keep it.

Sevda nodded. "I know it won't be easy, but it's what I want. What I've dreamed about since I realized that one day, I could have it all back. Not my family, but the life we had. I miss it."

"I miss what I had with my family, too." He offered her his hand as he stood, drawing her up with him. "I didn't realize how much I missed having company until I fished you out of the river."

She stepped into his arms and stood on her toes to kiss him. "I've never been so happy to see another person in my life. In case I haven't said it enough, thank you."

He let himself get drawn into her kiss, and for a few blissful moments the past stopped haunting him and he found himself at peace.

She's not staying and you can't leave, the part of him still thinking clearly reminded him, and he tore his mouth from hers. "I bet you're hungry. How long ago was your last meal?"

Her stomach rumbled loudly at the mere mention of food and he felt a pang of guilt that it hadn't occurred to him before now. "I had my last meal a few minutes before the ship got damaged."

"That was almost a day ago!" He turned and started back toward the cabin, then stopped and turned back to offer her his hand. "Let's get you fed."

SEVDA INDULGED HERSELF IN A LONG, hot shower after they returned to the cabin. Like everything else on her ship, the shower facilities were cramped and utilitarian. Raze's cabin, and his shower, were luxurious by comparison.

When she finally shut off the water and drew back the simple waterproof curtain, she discovered that Raze had left a fresh pair of thick, felted wool socks and a comb on top of the towel she had left out for herself. Beside the towel was the med-kit she had requested Eddi send to her.

She popped a pain-blocker, treated her cuts and bruises, and considered the man who had saved her life yesterday. She was drawn to him, but it wasn't only because of his looks, or the fact he'd saved her life. Maybe it was because they had things in common. More likely it was because she'd be leaving soon. Their time together had a built-in expiry date, so why not enjoy what time they had to the fullest?

Raze was stubborn and prickly, but she suspected that was a façade he used to push people away. If he really didn't care, he wouldn't have been around to pull her out of the water yesterday. He had walked all the way down to the valley floor to check on a total stranger during a dangerous storm. Whatever his reasons for living in complete solitude, it was obvious he believed it was necessary. She was something of an expert at keeping everyone at a distance, herself. At least, she had been.

By the time she had left the Torex orphanage, she had learned that the only one she could depend on was herself. No one could hurt or disappoint her if she didn't let them get close. It was safest to stay closed-off and self-reliant.

In the years she had been a scout, she'd slowly discovered that it didn't have to be that way. Sevda made friends with other pilots she crossed orbits with. Freighter jockeys and smugglers for the most part, but there were deep space mining crews and scouts like herself scattered across the galaxy.

They kept each other company on the long, dark voyages between the stars. When things went wrong, they did what they could to help, from rescuing marooned pilots to delivering spare parts. They watched out for each other, and they had shown Sevda that there were beings in the galaxy she could trust to have her back. Obviously, no one had ever been there for Raze.

She dressed quickly, spurred on by the tantalizing scent of breakfast. "Sexy, self-sufficient, mind-blowing lover, and he can cook. If only he wasn't such a pain in the ass, he'd be perfect." She barely got the door open before Raze spoke.

"I'm not even close to perfect, but I appreciate the compliment."

"How did you—*fraxx*, cyborgs have enhanced senses, don't they?"

He chuckled. "We do."

"You could have reminded me," she grumbled.

"But then I wouldn't have heard your compliment." He turned and gave her a slow, sexy smile that made her toes curl. "It's been a while since I've heard one of those."

"Try being nicer, you'll get more of them."

He gestured around the cabin. "From who? The AI on my ship doesn't have any personality subroutines. It flies the ship and does what I tell it."

"Wait. You have a ship? Where? Why didn't it show up on the scans?" She tried to remember what she could of the farm outside.

"Where did you think the hot water from your shower came from? Yes, I have a ship." He pointed his spatula to the wall to her right. "It's in a shielded building not far from the cabin."

"So that's how you have power and running water? I admit, I wondered."

"I have solar panels and a wind turbine for power, actually. I spent almost every bit of scrip that Torex gave me in back pay when they finally freed me."

She did a quick bit of math and uttered a low whistle. "How many years did you work...fight?" She tried to reorganize her words into something more accurate and decided to be blunt. "How long were you a slave?"

Raze's eyes widened. "I've never heard anyone come out and say it like that."

"Well, that's what you were. I might not matter to them, but at least they acknowledge that I'm a living being, with basic rights. You and the other cyborgs were considered property, not people. I can't imagine what that must have been like for you."

He moved a heavy metal pan off the stove, set down the spatula, and crossed the cabin to stand in front of her. "I was created very early. I left my maturation tank, underwent extensive testing, a little training, and then spent the next nine-plus years in combat. It was a nightmare I couldn't escape. There are still nights I jerk awake, convinced that I only dreamed that I was free."

She took his hand, and he drew her in close before wrapping his big arms around her shoulders. His head bowed over hers, and she found herself leaning into his strength, holding him as tightly as he was holding her. It didn't make any sense, but for some damned reason, Raze made her feel safe. More than that; she felt like she belonged. She hadn't felt like that since she'd lost her family and her home.

As she basked in the warmth of those feelings she indulged herself in a daydream where the two of them could have some kind of future together. It would never happen, of course, but it was a nice fantasy.

As if sensing her thoughts, Raze uttered a low curse and let go of her. "Breakfast is getting cold. Sorry."

He was gone a split-second later, leaving her feeling like someone had given her a teddy bear, then snatched it out of her arms the moment she hugged it. Somehow, she didn't think Raze would appreciate the suggestion that he was anyone's teddy bear. The thought made her grin.

"Can I help? It's been a few years since I cooked anything, but I can manage to set the table at least."

"Uh. Sure. Cutlery is in the top drawer to my left."

It only took a minute or two to set the table. There were only two sets of cutlery in the drawer, along with a collection of knives and other kitchen utensils that looked as well used as everything else she'd seen. It amazed her that he lived so simply when he had a ship parked only a few meters away.

"Hey, Bear. Anything else I can do?"

As expected, he reacted to his nickname with a stormy look. "Yeah, you can stop calling me that."

"Not going to happen. You keep calling me scout, I figured it was time to return the favor."

"Not the same thing." He pointed to her. "You are a scout. I am not a *fraxxing* bear, of any species."

"You're right. You're not a species of bear. You're a teddy bear. Big, snuggly. Fuzzy..."

"I'm not snuggly! Or fuzzy. You want something furry to snuggle, the noats are in their pen."

She laughed. Teasing Raze was fun, and it was one of the few ways she had found to get past his armor. "I recall you being pretty snuggly last night. And have you looked in the mirror lately? You're fuzzy, Raze. Beard, long hair, and all."

"Sev, I swear..." he growled something in a language she didn't recognize and finished plating their meal, making more noise than was necessary as he banged and slammed his way through the process.

Breakfast was delicious. After months of surviving on food-tabs and the simple meals her basic model food dispenser was capable of making, it was like eating at a five-star establishment. She was too busy eating to talk much, and Raze seemed content to let the silence stretch out between them.

It all felt so familiar. The rural setting, the simple cabin, the homecooked meal. This was what she wanted for herself someday. She envied Raze the life he'd carved out for himself. And she regretted that he was going to lose it all, soon. She hadn't told him, but from what she'd seen of the initial scans, this planet was rich in ores and minerals. Torex would be back, and they'd tear this idyllic world apart to get to the riches under the surface. This planet, and everything on it, was doomed.

6

It was while Raze was refilling their mugs with more coffee that Eddi broke the contented silence. "Pilot Rem, are you available for a status update?"

Her comm device was still by the bed, so she left the table to retrieve it.

"I'm here, Eddi. Relay update."

"I have located the cause of the power fluctuations and initiated repairs. Several couplings were damaged by the micro-meteors, which was causing intermittent connectivity issues in the—"

"I don't need the details. Just tell me that you can fix it."

"I already stated that I was fixing it. Are you receiving my transmission clearly, Pilot Rem?"

She rolled her eyes. "Yes, I am. Is there anything else you need from me right now? I'm having breakfast with Raze at the moment and would like to get back to my meal."

"Of course. I do have one inquiry before I terminate this transmission. Do you have any further information to add to the log regarding the presence of the undocumented humanoid lifeform known as Raze?"

"Nothing at this time. I'll update the record once I'm back onboard."

"Understood."

She turned off the comm device and set it back down on the side table.

"Undocumented lifeform?" Raze's gruff voice rumbled from across the cabin.

She turned to find him staring at her with a thunderous expression that would have made a Nantari rhino halt its charge and find somewhere else to be.

What the fraxx was he mad about? "Well, that's what you are, isn't it?"

"It's not nice to call the man who saved your life an undocumented lifeform."

"I didn't. Eddi did."

"You didn't correct her. I'm not a lifeform, scout. I'm the *man* you spent the night with."

Understanding dawned. "I know who and what you are, Raze. This isn't about you being a cyborg. I was trying to protect your privacy. Whatever Eddi knows, Torex will eventually know, too. Right now, all she has is your name. When I make my report, Torex is going to discover that you're trespassing on their planet. There isn't much I can do to protect you, but I can limit what information they start with."

His scowl deepened. "Do you have to tell them

about me at all?"

"Yes, I do. It's my job to scout planets and report my findings. That includes anything and anyone that could be a factor in their decision to mine a planet's resources."

He started to speak, but she held up a hand to forestall whatever grumpy thing was about to come out of his mouth. "Even if I didn't tell them, Torex would find out about you eventually. If that happened, they'd come after me for falsifying a report, and I could lose everything I've been working for. You of all people should know what it's like to work for the corporations. They don't tolerate anything less than complete obedience."

He placed their freshly filled mugs on the table but didn't sit down. "I saved your life. You're going to repay me by reporting me to Torex and letting them take everything I've built here?"

"It's not that simple." Sevda lifted her arms in an all-encompassing gesture. "This planet already belongs to them. Spoils of war and all that. They're not going to let it go just because you want to live here."

"Spoils of war?" Raze's voice rose to a roar. "Do you have any idea what you're talking about?"

Raze rounded the table and grabbed her wrist. "With me. Now."

He dragged her out into the yard in her stocking feet, ignoring her attempts to pull free. He strode down the middle of a muddy pathway, leaving her to scramble through the ooze to keep up. It didn't take long for the oversized socks to slide off her feet, leaving her barefoot.

"Yeouch! Will you at least slow down?" She finally demanded as she stepped on yet another rock hidden in the mud.

"What's wrong?"

She stuck out her mud covered foot and pointed to it. "No shoes, remember? You dragged me out of the cabin before I got to put any on. Not to mention I'm still feeling the effects of my little aquatic adventure in the flood yesterday."

"You still hurt from yesterday? I thought you took something for that?" he asked.

"Yes, but I'm still healing. I will be for another day or so. I'm not like you, Raze. I don't have a host of medi-bots swarming through my blood healing me up as fast as I get hurt. The pain-blocker helps, but not if I push myself too hard or get dragged around by a big, grumpy cyborg."

He growled in frustration. "I'm not grumpy!"

"Says the man growling at me." She curled her upper lip back, revealing her fangs as she uttered a guttural snarl back at him.

"Don't push me, scout. You're already on thin ice."

She drew herself to her full height and stood her ground. "Don't threaten me because I dared to tell you the truth. You can't stay here, Raze. If you do, you'll die."

"Then I'll die, because I'm not leaving." He didn't say another word, he simply scooped her into his arms like she weighed less than a noat and started back down the path. She could have protested, but what was the point? He wasn't going to relent until he'd shown her whatever they were going to see.

SHE WAS GOING to turn him in to Torex. He'd saved her life, and instead of thanking him, she was going to destroy everything. He shouldn't have let her get close.

"Where are we going?" she finally asked.

"I'm going to show you the price that was paid for this planet. Then, when you fly away and make your report to Torex, you'll truly understand what the *spoils of war* look like."

He had walked this path so many times in the past few years he could have navigated it blindfolded, but it took him longer than normal to cover the final stretch. He had never imagined there would be a moment he would share this place with anyone else.

The sun broke through the last of the clouds as he crossed through the final line of trees and entered a clearing, bathing the valley in light. The land here was covered with lush green grass and wildflowers. He had planted some of the flowers himself, adding to those that had already taken root here in the years he had been away. This is where he had buried his family. Twenty-one graves, each marked with a single stone with their names etched on a chiseled space.

"Graves?" Sevda asked, her voice hushed.

"My batch siblings."

"*Veth*. So many." She counted the stones aloud. "Twenty-one? Did you all come here after the war... or..." She looked up at him with dawning horror. "You were here during the war, weren't you? You lost your family fighting for this planet."

He set her down on the thick grass, keeping one arm wrapped around her as he belatedly realized he hadn't given her a chance to don a jacket, either. "There were twenty-six of us in the beginning. Three years later, I was the only one left. Twenty of my siblings are buried here."

"But there are twenty-one stones."

"That last one is for me."

She stared at him in confusion. "Why?"

"Because this is where my life ended. I might still be breathing, but I lost everything that made life worth living the day I buried the last of my family here."

She leaned into his side and sighed. "This is why you don't want to leave."

Now, maybe he could make her understand the need for her to protect this planet from destruction. "You see? This is why you have to help me. You can change the reports so they don't come back. If you don't help me, then Torex will take them from me all over again. I've given my life, my blood, and my family to them already. When will it be enough?"

"I don't know the answer to that. I don't know that there *is* an answer. The corporations do what they want and there's nothing we can do to stop it."

He pulled away from her. "Bullshit."

"Do you think I'd be doing this – working for them – if there was another way?" she demanded.

He jerked his thumb toward his chest. "Do you think I'd be here if that were true? They were going to kill us, scout. All of us. If we hadn't rebelled, I'd be dead. We took a risk, because it was the only chance we had. Now, the only chance I have is *you*."

Even as he said the words, he knew what her final answer would be. He could see it in her eyes. The scout he'd saved from drowning, the woman he had spent the night making love to—she was going to leave him to fight this battle alone.

SEVDA THREW her hands in the air in frustration. "You're not being reasonable! You keep seeing the world in black and white. There are more than two options for you. You could make another choice, Raze."

He scoffed and folded his arms over his chest. "What choice would you like me to make? Where could I go? I was created to be a soldier; a mindless killing machine that would obey every order without hesitation. I don't know how to be anything else. I don't fit in with anyone, anywhere."

"That's not true, you stubborn idiot! Look around you. You're not a killer anymore. You're a farmer. You have crops and livestock and a home you made yourself. As for where you'd go..." She softened her tone as she opened her heart. "You could come with me. We could work adjoining claims, help each other…"

"Why would I do that?"

Humiliation fueled her angry response. "Right. Because I'm just a one-armed, half-breed freak. I just thought that maybe going with me was a better choice than dying here. I want what you have. A farm. A quiet life. When I'm free of Torex, I'm going to make that happen. I was trying to show you there was another choice. But I guess there isn't, since you'd rather die than be with me."

He spat out his words through clenched teeth. "I told you, I can't leave. If you tell them about me, you'll be signing my death warrant."

"It's not that simple!"

"I think it is. You just don't want to make the hard choice."

For him, she might have. *Veth*, she had actually been tempted to try, but that was before he'd rejected her. "I can't do what you're asking, Raze. I don't think I could even if I wanted to. My ship records the scans automatically. I don't have access to those files. Everything is sent back to Torex for processing and review. Eddi knows you're here. I have to complete the scans, or my mission will be marked as incomplete, and I won't get paid."

"So it's about scrip now?" his voice was all acid and ice.

"No! *Fraxx*, you really don't think much of me, do you? I'm not selling you out. I'm telling you it's not possible. I can't protect you, or this place. This planet is going to be mined. You're going to die if you're here when that happens. Even if I destroyed Eddi and stranded myself here, that would only buy you a few months until they sent someone else to finish my mission."

He started to speak, but she cut him off.

"Don't worry, I'm not going to do that. You've made it clear how you feel about me. I don't want to stay where I'm not wanted. You're not the only one with plans, you know. You might think your life has ended, but I haven't even started to live yet. I've been indentured to Torex since I was thirteen. I want my life back."

"At what cost, scout? If you reclaim your life at the cost of my future, how are you any better than Torex?"

"What future?" She stormed across the clearing to stand over the final stone, the one meant for him. "You already carved your name on your headstone. That's not the act of a man who thinks he has a future."

"My future is here, with them."

"That's not a life. That's a life sentence. A short one."

"Why do you care?"

"I don't know. Clearly, that's a mistake on my part, since you care more about the *fraxxing* noats than you do about yourself or me."

Raze glowered at her. "I brought you here so that you'd understand why I can't leave this planet. If you're not going to help me, then there's no point in continuing this conversation. I'll take you back to the cabin."

"And if I want to continue talking about this? What if I want you to accept that this is not my fault?"

He looked down at her bare feet. "Then you'd have a long, uncomfortable hike back, alone."

"You are the most stubborn, difficult ass of a man I have ever met! I understand your reasons, but it doesn't change the facts. If you stay here, you *will* die."

"I'm not afraid of dying. My home is here. My family is here. I have to stay."

"No, you don't! I don't think you're afraid of dying at all. I think you're afraid of living."

"I'm not afraid of anything! Cyborgs don't feel fear. It's not part of our programming."

She folded her arms across her chest and snarled in frustration. "You're not a machine, Raze. You're a human being. We feel fear all the time, as well as guilt, and grief, and sorrow. Even half-breed freaks like me. Pain is part of living. I should know, I lost my entire family, too."

"Sevda..." he trailed off as if he didn't know what else to say.

"No. Don't say anything else. Just go. I'll find my own way back when I'm ready."

"I didn't..."

She cut him off with a sharp slash of her hand. "Go the *fraxx* away, Raze." She turned her back on him and started reading the names he'd chiseled into the other grave markers.

7

———

AFTER A MINUTE, Raze moved to the edge of the clearing and removed his socks and boots. He set them at the head of the trail where Sevda couldn't miss them. He would leave her here because she'd asked him too, but he wasn't going to make her walk back in bare feet. As she had already reminded him, she wasn't a cyborg. She couldn't block pain or heal quickly. Better she wore them for the walk back to the cabin.

He left and started making his way back up the trail, with Sevda's words playing over in his head every step of the way.

The walk didn't help clear his head. If anything, he felt more confused than ever. When he got back home, he took a quick shower to wash the mud from his feet, then dressed and started clearing away the breakfast dishes while he tried to put things in perspective. The situation was simple enough. They'd shared a night and a meal together, but that was all there could ever be. She had to leave. He had to stay. The end.

He grabbed a handful of river sand from the jar beside the sink and used it to scour the dishes clean. "I can't leave. My place is here. And what is she thinking, asking me to go with her? She barely knows me. She sure as hell doesn't know me well enough to say I'm staying here because I'm afraid."

Not that she'd want him to go with her after what he said. His words had hurt her, and for all his anger, that knowledge bothered him.

"Damn it," he muttered. This was why he preferred to be alone. The noats couldn't be hurt by a poorly chosen word. The chickens didn't care if he didn't speak for days. Even among his own kind he'd been considered a loner. His siblings were the only ones who understood him, and they were all gone.

He lapsed into silence, but inside his head, the diatribe went on unabated until the dishes were cleaned and put away. On a normal day, he'd leave the cabin to handle the day's chores. After a storm, the irrigation channels usually needed to be cleared of debris, and he still needed to check on the small orchard of fruit trees he was cultivating at the far edge of the farm.

Instead, he decided to tidy up the cabin. Sevda would be stuck here for another day at least, and she wasn't likely to want to sleep in bed with him tonight, not after everything they'd said to each other. With that in mind, he retrieved several blankets from their storage container beneath his bed and set them on the narrow couch that took up most of the living area wall. She'd have to curl up to fit, but it was more comfortable than the floor would be.

The cabin seemed too quiet without her laughing presence. After years of silence, he thought he'd be irritated by any sort of company. Instead, the quiet felt wrong.

"I'm losing my mind." He tossed a pillow onto the couch with more force than necessary. "Everything was perfect until that damned female arrived. Maybe she brought some kind of pathogen with her. One that my medi-bots can't fight."

An unexpected voice responded. "Pilot Rem does not carry any pathogens. If you are experiencing mental distress, the source will not be my pilot."

He spun around to glower at the comm device Sevda had left by the bed. "Eddi? Why are you eaves-dropping on me? And for the record, my distress is most definitely being caused by your damned pilot."

"Pilot Rem activated Sunrise Protocol. I am programmed to monitor this frequency continuously to ensure that there is no danger to her."

"So, you've been listening in since we got here?"

"Yes, Raze."

"*Fraxxing* wonderful. You must have gotten quite an earful."

"Technically, I do not have ears."

"I guess you don't. Did you record anything you listened to?"

"No. Recording only begins if I establish that my pilot is in danger."

"Thank the stars for that, at least. And for the record, your pilot is in no danger from me. You can deactivate Sunrise Protocol."

"You are not my pilot. I do not need to obey your directives. I will, however, verify with Sevda Rem if she wishes me to continue Sunrise Protocol upon her return. Do you think she'll be gone long? I would like to give her an update on my repairs."

"I have no idea how long your stubborn pilot will stay away. She's not very happy with me right now."

"She seemed happy with you last night."

He snorted. "We were both happier last night."

"I have been with Pilot Rem for more than four standard years. It is not common for her to be happy. She tells me that is because she won't be happy until she is free. You made her laugh, even though she will not be free until we finish this mission. Then she will no longer be indebted to Torex and can sell me to buy a place on a colony planet."

"Wait. Back up. She'll sell you? Don't you belong to Torex?"

"Torex requires all planetary scouts to purchase their own equipment, including a ship. Once a scout has worked long enough to pay off the basic equipment, they can upgrade again."

"And each time they upgrade their equipment, their debt to Torex increases again?"

"Yes."

It was another kind of slavery, one that forced the slave to sell themselves over and over again. He hadn't really understood how much control Torex had over Sevda's life. She'd told him, but he had still thought of her as an employee, someone who worked for the corporations by choice. He'd been wrong.

"If upgrading added to her debt load, why do it? Why not pay off what's owed and leave?"

"I am not sure I can answer your question. There are too many variables."

"Let me make it more specific, then. Why hasn't Sevda left Torex, yet? You, and the ship you control, are obviously not basic equipment."

"I am most definitely not basic. I am a Seeker Class vessel with advanced AI functionality. It took my pilot many years of work to be able to acquire me. I have the longest range of any scout ship model currently on the market. My pilot purchased me so that she could be assigned to the highest risk missions to outlying areas like this one."

He finally understood. "More risk, more pay? She bought you to be free sooner?"

"Yes. My pilot was indebted to Torex for both her upbringing and her cybernetic arm before she ever became a scout. To pay off her debts with lower risk missions would take another decade of her life."

"Thank you for explaining, Eddi."

"You are welcome, Raze. It is part of my programming to see to my pilot's health and wellbeing. The data I have collected indicate that you can make Sevda happy. Happiness is a desired condition that leads to wellness and stability."

He chuckled. "Are you matchmaking, Eddi?"

"I am merely explaining the logic behind my decision to speak with you about my pilot."

"Right. Of course, that's all you were doing. Thank you, Eddi. I'm going to find Sevda in a moment. I'll bring the comm device when I do, and I'll let her know you have an update."

"Thank you."

The cabin fell silent. It wasn't a comfortable silence, though. Something told him it would be a long time before he enjoyed quiet solitude again. He looked over at the blankets and pillow he'd set out for Sevda and frowned. He didn't want her to sleep somewhere else tonight. He wanted her with him.

He tossed the blankets back under the bed, put a fresh log on the fire, and headed out to find Sevda. He had no idea what he was going to say, but he had a feeling his first words should probably be an apology.

SEVDA DIDN'T TURN AROUND until she was certain Raze was gone. She didn't want him to see how much his rejection had hurt. It had been stupid to make the suggestion at all. They barely knew each other, but somehow... *Veth*, she had wanted him to say yes, but he hadn't. She was the only female on the whole planet; his only chance to live, and he'd chosen death instead.

Despite that, she still wanted to try and make him change his mind.

"I've lost my mind. That has to be it." She ran a hand over the rough edge of one of the grave markers. The name Talon was carved into the stone. She couldn't imagine how hard it must have been for Raze to carry each of his dead siblings up here and bury them. It must have taken days. Then, when the war had ended, he'd come back here to stay with the only family he had.

Her throat tightened, and a few stray tears welled up and spilled down her cheeks before she got herself back under control. She had only been able to visit her family's graves once. She had been sent to the city before they were buried, and once there, she hadn't been permitted to leave again until she turned seventeen. In the scant few days between her seventeen birthday and the day she was to report to Torex for training, she had made the journey and said her goodbyes.

She caressed the weatherworn stone beneath her hand. "He's never found a way to say goodbye to all of you, has he?"

Her only answer was the trill of birdsong and the whisper of the breeze through the branches of the trees that surrounded her.

It wasn't fair. They'd both given Torex so much of their lives already. It must have taken Raze years to establish himself here, working alone with no one but the noats and chickens for company. Now, he was going to lose everything again.

She wandered from grave to grave, paying her respects Raze's family. it wasn't her fault, but she was a cog in the machine that would descend on this place someday and disturb what should have been their final resting place.

"I'm sorry. I wish I could do more. I can't save this planet. I can't even save your brother. I tried, though. I'm just not what he wants. He'd rather die here with you than leave with me."

She finished her visitation and turned back toward the trailhead. There was only one way out of the clearing, so at least she wouldn't get lost. Part of her was tempted to take the path all the way back to the valley floor. Maybe the floodwaters had receded enough by now that she could get back onboard her ship and stay there until repairs were done. Her comm device was still at the cabin. She could use that to let Raze know she wouldn't be coming back. It would be easier than facing him again.

She was still contemplating her destination when she spotted the boots set neatly in the middle of the path. He'd taken off his shoes and left them for her so she wouldn't have to make the trek in bare feet.

"You are a complicated man," she muttered. Was this a peace offering? An apology? Or was he just being practical again? After considering things for a moment, she decided it didn't matter what his reasons were. She couldn't steal what had to be one of his few pairs of footwear, and as much as she didn't want to admit it, she couldn't make the trek to the ship in bare feet. She would have to go back to the cabin.

She slipped on the socks and boots, lacing them up as tight as they would go. They were still ridiculously oversized, but at least her feet wouldn't take a beating. She had enough cuts, bruises, and scrapes already.

She tromped through the trees and turned up the hill with a low groan. It hadn't seemed that far on the way down. Of course, the only times she'd been on this trail, Raze had been carrying her. It was easy to ignore the steep incline and increased gravity when someone else was doing all the work.

Still, the sun was shining, the air was clear, and the path was easy to follow. How many times had he traveled along it to pack the dirt so tightly? A hundred? A thousand? She mused as she walked, her thoughts whirling like the dust motes that danced in the sunbeams that streamed through the forest canopy above. Why leave the boots if he didn't care about her? And if he cared about her, why wouldn't he even think about leaving with her before Torex came?

She was still trying to make sense of his actions by the time the end of the trail came into sight. Before she made it to the top, though, Raze appeared. He descended the trail with his hands jammed into the pockets of his coat and an unreadable expression on his face. Neither of them said a word as they closed the distance between them.

When he was less than three feet away, he stopped

and planted his feet on the ground like he was preparing to block her. She came to a halt and tried to muster an indifferent expression. "Is this your way of telling me I should have gone with my plan to hike back to my ship and leave you in peace?" she asked.

"What? No. I was bringing you your comm device. Eddi wants to talk to you." He pulled her communicator out of his pocket and held it out to her. "And I, uh, I wanted to apologize."

"Thank you." she took back the offered item and slipped it into her pocket. "And thanks for the boots. You didn't have to do that."

He rubbed his knuckles along his jaw, and his cheeks actually darkened in a blush. "Yeah, I did. I dragged you down there, yelled at you, then left you with no way to get back safely."

"I was the one who told you to leave," she pointed out.

"You had your reasons. And uh, I'm sorry about that, too." He moved in closer and cupped her cheek in one calloused hand. "I don't think you're a freak, Sevda. I never did. Whatever else happens, I want you to know that."

She shrugged. "You wouldn't be the first one to think that. You won't be the last, either."

The corners of his eyes crinkled as he broke into a grin. "Now who's the grumpy one pushing people away?"

"You don't have a monopoly on that tactic, Bear." She hadn't meant to use the endearment, but her heart seemed determined to override her head. Or maybe that was just her libido.

"I don't want to push you away anymore. Odds are, you're going to be the last friendly face I ever see."

She nodded. "Even if I don't tell them about you, they're going to find you eventually. I understand why you don't want to leave, now. But I still think you're lying to yourself."

He scowled, but his thumb stroked across her cheek at the same time, lessening the impact of his stare. "You haven't been in my orbit that long, scout. What makes you think you know me better than I know myself?"

The truth spilled out of her in a torrent, her words as much a personal confession as they were an observation about him. "I know you. *Veth*, I've *been* you. You think you aren't worthy to be alive, that you don't have the right to every lungful of air you breathe because you didn't die when they did."

His eyes widened, but he didn't deny her words. "I wasn't there. I was scouting a way out of the valley when the attack came. By the time I made it back, they were all dead. My entire unit. My family. Gone."

She lifted her hand to cover his. "But it wasn't your fault. Just like it wasn't mine that my family died in that fire and I didn't. We're still here, and they're not, and it hurts."

He nodded.

"You're not going to tell me I'm wrong? No arguments?" she asked softly.

"No arguments. You're even smarter than you are stubborn, did you know that?"

"Was that you trying to flirt?" she teased.

"Maybe. I've never actually tried before."

The look she gave him was one of incredulous shock. "Never?"

He shook his head. "When I was in combat, I didn't need to flirt. The female cyborgs were uh...accommodating. It was part of their programming, and none of us could reveal that we were self-aware."

"But the wars ended years ago. I mean, you never..."

"Not until you."

"You really have been determined to punish yourself, haven't you?"

"Says the woman who flies the riskiest missions she can find to earn enough money to start a new life somewhere. You don't get to start that life if you die trying to buy your freedom, you know."

"How did you know about that?"

"I had a chat with Eddi while you were out here."

Sevda wrinkled nose. "That *fraxxing* AI talks too much."

"Maybe. But I'm glad she did." He leaned down and brushed his lips against hers, and she threw her arms around him, rising on her toes to kiss him back.

It was so much easier to stay mad at him when he was doing all he could to push her away. When he was being vulnerable and sweet and kissing her, her resistance melted faster than a snowball in a supernova.

"So, we're not fighting anymore?" she asked.

"I don't want to fight with you. There are better things we could be doing with the time we have left." He kissed her again, his hand sliding into her hair as he made love to her mouth with a single-minded focus that made her toes curl.

"We could have more time if you agreed to come with me and start again somewhere new."

He groaned. "I made a promise to them. After they were all buried, I promised them I would be back someday, and that I wouldn't leave again."

There was so much pain trapped in his words that her heart bled. "Raze, do you really believe that you'd lose them if you left? Your siblings aren't here on this planet." She laid her hand on his chest. "They're in here. We can't leave the ones we lost. We take them with us no matter where we go."

He lifted his hand to cover hers. "They were all I had."

"Well, now you have me. I don't have many friends, but I keep the ones I have."

"Friends?" He lifted his head, revealing brown eyes full of heat. "We're more than friends, aren't we?"

"I don't know what we are. We can't stop fighting long enough to get that far."

"We're done fighting. At least, I hope we are." He released her and took a step back, then took her hand. "How about we talk instead? I want to know more about you than what little Eddi shared. Friends do that, right?"

"Yeah, they do. Why don't you show me what you've built here, and we'll talk." She squeezed his hand and let him lead her up the hill to the plateau. She was determined to use what time they had left to convince him to come with her.

8

RAZE KEPT Sevda's hand in his as they toured the farm. He showed her everything. His ship, the greenhouses, the shed where he kept his tools, and the cool, earth-scented root cellar he'd dug behind the cabin where he stored whatever bounty his harvest yielded each year.

"And this is my orchard. It's still a long way from being mature, but it's finally starting to produce enough I can't eat my entire harvest in one meal."

"Raze, those trees. How long." She paused and pointed to the orchard. "How long have they been growing?"

"About five years, now." He frowned. "Is there something wrong? Should they be bigger? I've never actually seen an apple tree."

"Wrong? No. There's nothing wrong. They're thriving here. I just – it never really sank in until now how long you've been here, and how much you've accomplished."

"I didn't have anything else to do." Building this place into a home had been the driving focus of his life for years. It kept him busy enough that he didn't have time to be lonely, or think too much about what he'd lost.

Sevda was still looking around, chewing on her lower lip as she pondered something.

"What is it?"

"I need to ask Eddi to clarify something for me." He stayed silent as she pulled out the comm device. "Eddi, I need you to look something up for me."

"Hello, Pilot Rem. I have an update for you on the repair—

"Not now, Eddi. This is important. Review the Unified Galactic Agreement rules for colonizing a planet and confirm that this planet is currently available for colonization claim."

"Pilot Rem, I can confirm that based on current law, it would be possible for a colonization claim to be filed if the proper criteria have been fulfilled."

Raze's head was spinning. He hadn't planned on colonizing anything. He just wanted to live here in this valley in peace.

"Eddi, what are the proper criteria?"

"The criteria are extensive, but the key elements are as follows. Colonists must have supported themselves for a period of four years on the planet's surface without any support from outside sources, including eighty-five percent of all food consumed. If at the end of four years, they have proven to be self-sustaining, they can file for colony status."

Sevda turned to look at him. "How long have you been here?"

"More than four years."

She beamed. "And you never left the planet at all, right? And I was your only visitor?"

"Right." He nodded, dazed.

"Eddi, please scan Raze's entire holdings and compare to all criteria. Determine if there is a likelihood that Raze has met all criteria for colonization."

There was a brief pause. "I estimate a ninety-eight percent chance that is the case, Pilot Rem."

Raze tried to wrap his head around what was happening. "Did you just figure out a way for me to stay here?"

"I think so. A legal, non-rule breaking way."

He hauled her into his arms and hugged her until she gave a grunt of protest.

"Ribs!"

"Sorry." He eased his grip but didn't let go. "Thank you."

"There are no guarantees this will work. I'm betting you're going to be sick of paperwork before this is over, and they might reject your claim, but…"

"But there's a chance I can stay here." He slipped a finger under her chin and lifted her head so he could look her in the eyes. "And so could you."

Her haunting, multi-hued eyes shimmered with tears. "Yeah?"

"Yeah. But not adjoining plots."

"Oh. Of course. You want to keep this valley for yourself. That makes sense."

He stroked his calloused thumb over her soft cheek. "No, sweetling. I want you to think about staying here, in this valley, with me."

"But I have to leave," she pointed out.

"And this isn't a colony planet, yet. We've both got work to do, scout."

"You're sure? Yesterday you were planning on spending the rest of your life alone."

"Yesterday, I didn't have you."

The smile she gifted him with made his heart overflow with emotions he had almost forgotten existed. Happiness. Affection. Hope. "I knew the cranky loner thing was an act. I like this version of you much better."

"Yes, yes. You're very smart, sexy, and amazing. And yet, you still haven't agreed to my offer. When you're free of Torex, will you come back here, to me?"

She tipped her head into his hand and nuzzled his fingers before answering. "Only if you promise me that if you can't get approved for colony status, you'll come with me instead of staying here to die with the planet."

"Leave?"

"Not leave. Live."

He looked around at the home he'd made for himself, then back at the woman in his arms. For most of his life, he had simply existed. Sevda was offering him a chance to have a life. For a moment, he thought he heard the voice of his siblings whispering on the breeze. *Say yes.*

He wasn't ready to commit to leaving. Not yet. So instead of agreeing, he asked, "Can I bring the noats?"

Her laughter filled the orchard. "They go on *your* ship."

"Fair enough."

"Is that a yes?" she asked.

"It's as much as I can give you right now."

She rose up on her toes to kiss him. "Then I'll take it. For now."

He lifted her into his arms and kissed her back. He'd renounced the world once, and she'd brought it all back to him. Even if he wanted to, he didn't think he had the strength to turn his back on everything again. Not if he'd have to give up her, too.

He loved the way her curves pressed into him and the way her kisses tasted of cinnamon. It was a flavor that he suspected he would quickly become addicted to. Her short, blue-black hair was like silk in his hands, and her laughter warmed the coldest recesses of his heart. It wasn't love. Not yet. But what burned between them was so much more than lust, or a need to end their loneliness.

He carried her to one of his favorite spots; a stretch of flat, grass-covered ground beneath the limbs of the largest tree in his orchard. It was indigenous to the planet, and once he had discovered that the fruit was edible, he'd transplanted several of the trees.

"Where are we going?"

"My thinking spot."

"What do we need to be thinking about right now?"

"We have a lot of things to consider, and plans to make, but right now it's the closest place I can think of where I can get you naked again."

She laughed and nipped at his lower lip. "Outside?"

"Cabin's too far away."

"I think you might be the perfect man for me."

"I'm not a man. I'm a cyborg."

"In case you've forgotten, technically, so am I." She stroked his cheek with her artificial arm.

"So you are. And a very sexy one, at that."

He crouched beneath his favorite tree and laid her down in the sweet grass.

"This is nice." She stretched out indulgently, back arched, arms over her head. It was enough to test the limits of his control.

He pulled his shirt over his head and tossed it aside. "Clothes off. Now."

She stuck out her tongue at him. "Words good. Use more."

"Scout..." his voice dropped to a low growl of warning.

"Yes, Bear?"

He shed his pants in seconds and dropped to his knees at her side. "Time's up."

"These are your clothes. Do you have enough left to tear this to shreds, too?"

"Don't care." He had her undressed in less than a

minute, spurred on by needs and desires that he could barely control.

"I'm going to need to go shopping for you before I come back, here, aren't I?"

"Or we can make this valley a clothing optional area."

Her eyes widened. "You're making jokes now? Who are you and what did you do with my grumpy bear?"

"Your bear is right here, sweetling." He stopped any further comments with a kiss that made her moan and writhe beneath him. How had he ever thought that he could be happy alone?

SEVDA LET GO of everything but this moment. Plans for the future, hopes, and fears and considerations all faded away as she let herself get lost in the fire that burned between them.

He had finally shown her the man behind the mask, and he was everything she suspected, and more. This was a man she could love someday. She knew it.

Their tongues tangled as he moved over her and wedged a knee between her thighs. The hairs on his chest rubbed against her breasts, and the sensation made her nipples go diamond-hard in seconds. She arched against him, pressing their bodies together as she speared her hands into his long hair and kissed him deeper. His beard tickled, and she knew she'd end up with whisker burn before they were done. She didn't care. In fact, she liked the idea of wearing his marks, even if it was only temporary.

He kissed his way down her body, devouring her an inch at a time. When he reached her breasts, she drew his head in closer, and he complied with her silent demand by closing his mouth over one taunt nub and sucking hard. A jolt of pure need sizzled from his mouth to her clit, making her arch against him again. His fingers closed over her other nipple, stroking and tugging it until she was half-wild with need and aching for more.

As he moved lower, she raised her head to watch, admiring the powerful build of his body and the way his size dwarfed hers. She'd always been too big. Too thick. Too tall. But not with him.

He reached her navel and circled it with the tip of his tongue. "Open for me."

She parted her thighs, the movement crushing more of the sweet smelling grass that cushioned her. She'd never made love outside, with the sky overhead and the sun streaming through the leaves to mark them both with dappled light. It was decadent and wonderful, and she wished with all her heart that somehow, they'd be able to stay here and make a life together. What kind of life that would be, only time would tell.

"Stop thinking, scout." He parted her folds with his calloused fingers and pressed his mouth to her pussy. After that, she couldn't have held a thought in her head if she wanted to. Pleasure bloomed deep inside her, sending her senses soaring.

He teased her with light flicks of his tongue, never using enough pressure to let her come. His fingers slid into her channel, filling her with slow, steady thrusts that made her tremble.

She raised her legs, planting her feet on the ground so she could raise her hips higher, pushing against his mouth until he finally gave her what she craved. He drew her throbbing clit into his mouth, working it with tongue and suction until she shattered into a thousand bliss-filled pieces.

When she opened her eyes again, he had risen to his knees and was watching her with a self-satisfied expression on his handsome face.

"You know, some ancient religions on Earth used to believe that making love in the fields would help the land become fertile and increase their harvests. I think we should make that a tradition for our future colony."

She laughed and crooked her finger at him, beckoning him closer. "How about a tradition just between us?"

He moved over her, slanting a torrid kiss to her lips before answering. "I like that idea even more. Every spring we'll do this at least once. And when the day comes you don't meet me out here, I'll know our time is over."

She slid her hands into his hair and gripped tight, forcing him to look at her. "I'm not sure what the future holds for us, but I don't see a day when I don't want to do this with you. Not until I'm old and gray and you're still…"

She stopped talking and kissed him. She didn't want to think about the fact that while he was more or ageless, she wasn't.

"Hey, none of that. We're not talking right now, remember?" he settled his big body between her legs. "Two days ago I thought I'd die without ever seeing another being. One day ago you arrived and told me I was going to lose my home. Today, you came up with a way to save it, and me. Who knows what tomorrow will bring?"

She kissed her way along the chiseled line of his jaw, loving the way the rasp of his beard felt against her face. "And there you go, being sweet again. If you keep this up, I'm going to end up loving you, and then where will we be?"

His brown eyes widened, and his face broke into a smile so bright it rivaled the sun. "*Veth*, I hope to find out."

"Me, too."

He groaned and pressed his cock to her entrance. "Say it again, Sevda."

"I'm going to love you someday, Raze."

He buried himself inside her, his gaze never leaving hers. "I hope someday comes soon."

"Me, too." She watched his expression as he claimed her. There was a tenderness in his eyes she hadn't seen before, and the promise of something deeper.

He withdrew slowly, then powered into her with enough force to make her moan. She released his hair and let her hands fall to his shoulders, holding onto him as he took her with a passion that blazed so hot it threatened to burn her alive.

His lips found hers as they came together, hips pumping, breaths ragged, hearts racing. His cock stroked deep inside her, igniting desires and flooding her with so much pleasure she was almost drunk with it.

Her nails raked across his skin as a primal force tore through her. She pulled away from his kiss and raised her head to sink her fangs into the muscle of his shoulder. He hissed and fucked her harder, the two of them locked together as they reached the apex of their climb.

His cock thickened and jerked and the orchard rang out as he cried out her name as his orgasm hit. His wild, shuddering thrusts pushed her over the edge shortly afterward, and time slowed, allowing her to enjoy the moment one pleasure filled heartbeat at a time.

As reality slowly returned, Raze withdrew, shifted to one side and stretched out beside her. She snuggled in close, and he draped an arm around her waist, holding her to him. "How long will you have to be gone?"

"Too long." She sighed. "At least another month, possibly longer. That's just for the mission. Then, I have to wait to get my scans verified and wait again for them to process my payment and my request to end my contract. It could be three or four months before I can come back here. I'll have to ask Eddi for a more accurate estimate."

"Two standard months, twenty-eight days," Eddi's muffled voice came from under the pile of their clothes.

"Eddi! Why are you still monitoring me?"

"Because you have not deactivated Sunrise Protocol. Might I suggest you do so? It's apparent that Raze is not a threat."

Raze chuckled. "I forgot to tell you about that."

"Oh. Oh, *fraxx*." Sevda blushed. "You aren't recording, are you, Eddi?"

"Raze made the same inquiry. No, I have not been recording."

"You can deactivate Sunrise Protocol, Eddi.

"Confirmed."

"But since you were listening. Do you really think we can get back here in three months?"

"I have been referencing my astronavigation software. If we depart in three days' time, there is a window that will allow us to decrease our time in system by a week or more. I have replotted the rest of our journey as well. I know you do not appreciate it when I backseat drive, however, this time I thought it prudent."

"I don't know if she appreciates it, Eddi, but I do. Thanks."

"You are very welcome, Raze."

"Don't encourage her, Bear. I have to deal with her for the next three months, you don't."

"She's given us an extra day together, and she's going to bring you back to me faster than you thought. I'm very thankful." He reached up to cup her breast in one hand. "I'm going to miss you."

"You're going to be too busy doing paperwork and filing claims to miss me much. And that's before you consider all the work you do around here. I'll be back before you know it."

He blew in her ear. "And we're going to talk every day, right? There's still so much I don't know about you."

The suggestion made her heart do a happy triple-beat with a somersault at the end. "We'll talk. It would be nice to have someone to talk to every day besides Eddi. I bought her some personality upgrades before this mission, which is why she's so damned quirky now. I was hoping for a better conversationalist, but I got a nag, instead."

"Oh, she's not so bad. She helped me see a few things I was missing. She takes her job of making sure her pilot is safe and happy very seriously. She can keep that job until you come back here."

"And then what?" she asked.

"Then, I'm hoping that keeping you safe and happy becomes my job. We'll need to find a new task for your AI."

"She can help you run the colony. That should keep her busy."

"Run the—*Fraxx*, no. I just live here." The look of panic on his face made her laugh.

"If you file the paperwork, you're going to be doing more than just living here. You'll have to be the leader, at least while things are getting set up."

"Leader?"

"Of the colony, Bear. Try to keep up. If this is a colony planet, eventually there will be others here. That's part of the deal."

He exhaled sharply. "Other people. *Fraxx*."

"They don't have to live here, in your valley. In fact, given the flooding issue, I think it's best we pick another location. Maybe where the river leaves the valley?"

"Maybe. There's good land there. Plenty of room to build."

"You'd only have to lead them for the first year or so. We'll have to stay with them, though. Help them adjust and get settled. You know this planet. The weather, the seasons, the animals and plants. They're going to need your help."

He hugged her to him and sighed. "They're going to need *our* help. I might know this planet, but people...I don't know much about them at all."

"I'll teach you. I know this isn't exactly what you wanted, but it beats losing it all, doesn't it?"

He nodded, still mulling things over. "But not in this valley."

She laughed. "Right. Not in this valley. This place is just for us."

"And after a year of helping, we come back here to stay," he insisted

"We'll figure this out. I'm not leaving for another three days. We've got time to make a plan." Planning was something she was good at. Setting goals and finding ways to reach them had been what pulled her out of her grief at losing her family. Making plans for her future had kept her moving forward no matter how hard things got.

Now she had a new plan, and his name was Raze. He'd offered her the one thing she wasn't sure she could have found anywhere else: acceptance.

Raze chuckled. "I had a plan. Come here. Live quietly. Never leave. Then you came along. Since you ruined that, I think it's only fair you help me make a new one."

"Your plan sucked. Ours will be better."

He pressed a kiss to the top of her shoulder. "I think everything's going to be better, now."

Lying in the grass, wrapped up in the arms of her lover and with a new future ahead of them, Sevda had to agree. Things were finally looking up, for both of them.

EPILOGUE

RAZE WALKED out of the cool, dim sanctuary of the barn and shielded his eyes against the glare of the late summer sun. The heat was harsh enough he had released the noats from their pen for the last few days so they could take refuge in the orchard, where the trees offered some shade.

The crate he carried contained the last of the corn he used to feed the livestock over the winter months. He set it down with the others. Over the last week, he had started to accept that he would have to leave this place. Torex had challenged his claims, retaliating with lengthy legal arguments and strongly worded warnings to vacate the planet immediately.

Sevda's scans had revealed this world was rich in ores and minerals, and the mining corporation wanted to tear the planet to pieces in order to get to them. Before that happened, he would be gone, taking with him a few saplings of his favorite fruit trees and his herd of noats. Soon, they'd be the only things left of this place.

He'd been angry at first. Enraged that Torex was taking even more of his life in the name of profit, but as the days passed, he'd let go of his anger and found acceptance. He wouldn't have been able to do it without Sevda. Even though she'd been gone for almost three months, she'd become more ingrained in his life with every passing day.

They talked daily, usually in the evenings after they'd both eaten their dinners. She'd adjusted time aboard her ship to synchronize their days. He'd learned so much about her since she had left. He knew her favorite food was something called a meringue, and that her nose crinkled whenever she was irritated. He also knew that she was the only being in the universe whose laughter always made him feel better about things. Each night she'd blow him a kiss before signing off, and he couldn't wait for the day that he could have her back in his arms again and kiss her for real. He'd even trimmed his beard for her, because she had mentioned that it tickled when he kissed her.

In two days, they'd be together again. Time had never passed so slowly. Every time he walked outside, he'd catch himself looking up at the sky, hoping to see her ship.

He went back inside the barn. He was done packing for the day, but there were still chores to do. He checked the water levels in the chicken coop, then took a few minutes to gather up the eggs from the nesting boxes and set them in the basket he used to carry them to the cabin each day.

Sevda was bringing as many supplies as she could fit on board, and he was looking forward to being able to restock his pantry with staples like flour and sugar again. Maybe they could use some of the eggs to make a cake or cookies or maybe even those meringue things. He had no idea how to bake, but the idea suddenly appealed to him. He wanted to do something to mark her return –that is, once he let her out of bed.

He finished collecting the day's eggs and set off for the cabin. He barely got beyond the barn doors though, when the noats started bleating in agitation.

"What's got you wooly-faced fools in a tizzy this time?"

Several of the grazers came charging out of the orchard, eyes wide with fear as they made straight for the barn. Was there a predator on the prowl? He doubted it. If there were, all of the noats would be hightailing it inside by now. They weren't the brightest beasts, but they had good instincts when it came to staying alive.

A few more noats appeared at the edge of the orchard, all of them staring up at the sky. He turned and looked, too, and grinned when he saw a slash of white standing out against the blue. A ship's contrail, followed by a glint of silver. He grinned and called out to the animals. "We've got company!"

He kept half an eye on the descending ship as he

quickly set aside the eggs and filled a bucket with grain. He rattled it loudly enough for the noats in the orchard to hear. Recognizing the sound, they came trotting across the yard and into the barn. He had them secured inside before the comm device in his pocket started to chirp. He fished it out, still grinning.

"You told me you weren't going to be here for two more days, scout. Everything okay?"

"I missed you, you big, grumpy bear, so I burned a little more fuel and got here early. Is it safe to land behind the cabin? I saw you putting the noats in the barn."

"You're good. I cleared more space back there so you should have plenty of room."

"Then I will see you when I land. I've got some news to share."

"I don't care about news. I'm just glad you're back."

He was whistling as he closed up the barn and jogged toward the landing area he had cleared for her.

The sleek scout ship made a perfect landing, far different from the drunken approach it had made the last time it touched down on this planet.

The door opened almost immediately, and Sevda hopped down before the ramp had finished extending.

Veth, she looked good. Her blue-black hair gleamed in the sun, and she was wearing a white sleeveless top that clung to her curves and showed off a tantalizing amount of golden skin. He opened his arms and she ran to him, throwing herself into his embrace with enough force to make him take a half-step backward even as he lifted her into his arms.

"Hello, sweetling."

"Hey, Bear. Miss me?"

He barely managed to answer her before his lips crashed down on hers. "Yes."

She wrapped her legs around his hips and kissed him back, mouth open, her hands buried in his hair. The air damn near sizzled with the heat coming off of them, and he swore to himself that whatever happened, he would never let Sevda fly out of his life again.

He turned and started walking toward the cabin. "Where are we going? I've got a ship full of stuff we need to unpack."

"Why bother? We're not staying here. No sense in unpacking everything but a few staples."

She started to laugh. "Who says we're not staying?"

"Torex." He stopped walking to stare down at her beaming face.

"I know something you don't know," she sang the words with glee. She cupped his scarred cheek in her hand. "We're staying, Raze. The colony is approved. All you have to do is sign an agreement with the IAF, and we can stay forever."

That didn't make any sense. "What's the Interstellar Armed Forces have to do with colonization?"

"Usually, nothing. This is a special arrangement. I don't know the details, yet. I think they're classified.

They said they'll explain before you agree to anything, though. When it started to look like Torex was going to win, I talked to some friends of mine, looking for advice. One of them has connections with the right people, and here we are."

"Who are the right people? I'm sorry, sweetling, but I'm still trying to catch up here."

She laughed. "I know. And I only got the message last night after we talked, so I don't know much more than I already told you. My friend's name is Phyl Harrington, and she's a cargo pilot out on the Drift. As it turns out, she's friends with a group of cyborgs that live there, and somehow, that wily old smuggler has made friends with some high ranking IAF officers, too. *Veth*, There's so much I need to tell you. All of it good news. Amazing news, actually. If you say yes, they'll even dose me with medi-bots. Can you believe it?"

"They can do that?"

She nodded, beaming. "Phyl negotiated it as part of the deal."

"You have amazing friends." He couldn't believe what she was telling, not really.

"I do. And they can't wait to meet you. Phyl's already making plans to drop by, and she'll bring whatever else we might need when she comes."

"We can really keep this place, and I can have you with me forever?"

"Forever. All you have to do is sign."

His heart soared, and he spun her around in a

circle before kissing her again. "Forever sounds good to me."

"Me too."

He stared at her, amazed at how much change she'd brought into his life. Now that she was back, it was as if the sun had come out from behind the clouds, and everything was vibrant and warm again.

"What's that look for?" she asked, her brow furrowing.

"I love you, and I'm happy you're home."

Her eyes widened, and her lips parted, but it took several heartbeats before she said anything. "I love you, too."

That was the moment that everything clicked into place. He had a home, a future, and a woman who loved and accepted him. This was the life he used to dream of years ago, before everyone he cared for and everything he wanted was stripped away. She'd done that. She'd filled his home, his heart, and his life with hope.

"Marry me."

"Yes." She covered his face with kisses. "Yes, yes, yes!"

"Then I guess we better agree to the IAF's deal. It's the only way I can think of to get someone here to marry us." He started walking toward the cabin again, and this time she didn't argue. Instead, she laid a trail of kisses from his neck to his ear, then started nibbling on his earlobe.

"You keep that up, we're not going to make it to the cabin, scout."

"You've figured out my cunning plan." She nipped his ear with one delicately pointed fang. "Just one thing I need to know, first."

It was getting hard to think, but he managed to grunt one word. "What?"

"Where's here? This planet needs a name."

He lifted her higher in his arms and looked around them, and the name came to him in the distant voices of his absent batch siblings. "Welcome to planet Liberty."

"Liberty." She spoke the name with reverence. "That's perfect."

"And so are you. When you crash landed here, I wanted you gone as fast as possible. Now, I never want you to leave."

"That's good because Eddi has informed me she's not taking off again unless it's a dire emergency. She seems to think I should stay, too."

"Remind me to thank her...later." They reached the door of the cabin and he hip-bumped it open without putting her down. So much had changed since the first time he'd carried her through these doors.

"You were the last thing I expected to find when I landed here. Eddi's miscalculation was the luckiest break of my life. I thought she was going to ruin my chances of getting free of Torex and starting the next stage of my life on schedule. Instead, she found me a home." There were tears in her eyes as she smiled up at him. "I'm finally home."

He kissed her tears away. "We're both home, sweetling. We made it." After years of loneliness, they'd both found what they were looking for. Each other.

THE END

No Limit - The Drift Book 5
Releasing May 15th, 2018

Three hearts. Two worlds. No limits.

Tyran and Ket are on a mission. Find an inhabitable planet. Start a new colony. Escape the archaic rules and traditions of the Vardarian homeworld. They never expected to find their mate along the way, and they never imagined she'd be a diminutive human female with pink hair and a warrior's spirit.

Phaedra Kari has been called a lot of things in her life: trouble, cyber-jockey, lunatic, hacker, but never someone's mate - not until an alien prince and his best friend arrive at the Drift. She's got plans of her own and they don't include mating anyone, not even a pair of gorgeous aliens whose every touch tempts her to say yes.

When corporate backstabbing progresses to real-life murder, these three will need to come together to ensure the survival of their plans, their friends, and each other.

Pre-Order it Today

CHAPTER ONE

Ket heard Tyran stomping up to the door to the observation lounge, each boot fall landing in time to a litany of decidedly unprincelike curses. Being away from court had been good for Tyr, even if the boredom was slowly driving them both insane.

"Ket! How many times do I need to tell you to quit switching the gravity orientation in the corridors? I just slammed my head on the ceiling, again."

Ket was floating several feet above his favorite chair as he reviewed the latest data from the long-range scans on a wall monitor. The observation lounge was one of the few rooms on the ship big enough to allow him to stretch his wings.

"Sorry. I forgot to switch that back after I was done."

"Done what? Why did you need to be walking on

the ceiling? And why are you floating? Something wrong with the furniture?" Tyr was annoyed enough that his skin was a brilliant shade of silver. For anyone else, that would have been a warning to step carefully, but Ket had been the prince's *anrik*, his blood-bound brother and protector, since Tyr was ten years old.

"There's nothing wrong with the furniture. I was just looking for a change in perspective." The only thing wrong with the furniture was that he'd seen it every day for more than three months. In that time, Ket had explored every inch of the ship. There wasn't a chair, bed, or room he hadn't spent time in. When he had agreed to Tyr's suggestion that they escape from the Imperial Court and go on this scouting mission, it had sounded exciting. Finding a new world to colonize would be an adventure. Only they had yet to find a single inhabitable world, and instead of adventure they faced a daily grind of dull routine.

"As for what I was doing that required me to flip the gravity, I was repairing a power conduit. It was easier to swap gravity than find a ladder."

"Next time, change it back. There's nothing fun about stepping into a corridor only to discover up and down have been reversed." Tyr rubbed the top of his head, making his short, black hair stand up in unruly spikes.

"That depends on your point of view. To me? That's funny. I'm sorry I missed it."

"In that case...."

Without warning, Ket dropped out of the air like a

stone and landed in a sprawled heap of wings and limbs across the unsuspecting chair he'd been floating over. "*Baka*. That was uncalled for."

Tyran snorted with laughter. "I thought it was funny. Must have been my point of view."

Ket flicked two of his fingers up in an obscene gesture before retracting his wings and arranging himself more comfortably in his chair. "Point taken. Next time I'll put it back."

"Thank you." Tyr entered the lounge and Ket took note of the fact his friend was wearing one of his more formal garments. The sleeveless vest had a ring of gemstones affixed to the collar, and the flowing fabric was dyed in green and black, the traditional colors of the Varosa royal family.

"Did you find anything of interest on the scans?" Tyr claimed a seat near one of the floor-to-ceiling windows that gave a breathtaking view of the galaxy outside.

They were currently light-years from any star system, surrounded by the velvet blackness of deep space. The stars gleamed like distant gems, and in orbit around one of them had to be the planet they were searching for. If they found it, they could escape the demands of the imperial court and the Vardarian empress, Tyran's twin sister, Neha.

"Maybe." Ket visualized the data he wanted and the nanites that filled his body linked to the ship's computer. A hologram of the area where scans had showed something out of the ordinary appeared in the air in front of him a second later.

"What am I looking at?"

"A map," Ket retorted.

"I'm not in the mood for your jokes, Ket. What's so special about the area in this map?"

Ket reached up and manipulated the image, expanding it and then zeroing in on a sector. "The scans are picking up some kind of signal from this area. It could be more cosmic noise or a natural phenomenon, but the computer projects a sixty percent likelihood it's not naturally occurring."

Tyr leaned forward, his hands on his knees as he stared at the display. "Sixty percent?"

"It could be another pulsar, or a star nursery, but it's the strongest lead we've had in weeks. If there's intelligent life over there, I vote we go find them. I'm dying for a conversation with someone I haven't known for most of my life. You already know all my best stories."

"Agreed. I caught myself having a long, in-depth conversation with one of the servo-droids this morning. Let's go see what's making all that noise. Where there's life, there have to be life-supporting planets."

"That's the theory." Ket took another look at his friend and frowned. There was something more bothering Tyr than just a bump on the head. "I know that look. And that outfit. You've been speaking with your sister, haven't you?"

He nodded. "She wants me to stop this 'frivolous pursuit' and return home."

"You've been at her side her entire life. She doesn't understand why you're not there, now, giving her your counsel and support."

Tyran shook his head, and the light in his green eyes dimmed for a moment. "Neha doesn't value my counsel. She wants me close, so she can ensure I don't act against her."

"You've never been disloyal to her. Why does she persist in her belief to the contrary? It's ludicrous. Everyone who knows you is fully aware that you have no desire to be emperor." Ket pointed to the stars outside. "Otherwise you'd be on the damned throne instead of roaming uncharted space."

"She is the eldest. It would be dishonorable for me to even consider trying to claim what is her birthright."

"She's only older than you by a handful of minutes. There were many who felt you had the right to challenge her." His green eyes narrowed. "And before you get defensive, remember that I'm not one of them. I'm simply pointing out the facts."

"I know. Your loyalty is not in question, my brother."

"Did she order you to return?"

"Not yet. But she will, soon. Those *vipa* she calls her counselors have fed her so many lies that she no longer trusts anyone but them. Even our mother has lost most of her influence. We are running out of time."

And if they returned without finding what they

were looking for, they would never get another chance. Declaring a diaspora and leading a group of colonists to a new home would allow them both to live free. For Tyran, that meant escaping a life full of court intrigue and his sister's influence. For Ket, it meant being away from those who would judge him for his ancestry. He wasn't a pure-blooded Vardarian.

Anywhere else in the empire, that would be the norm. Their species had scattered across the stars centuries ago, finding new worlds to inhabit, new alliances to forge, and occasionally finding races that were genetically compatible with them. But Ket lived on the Vardarian homeworld, where everyone was judged by their lineage instead of their actions.

Tyr got to his feet and walked over to the hologram. He touched the location with one finger and a set of coordinates appeared about it. A moment later, the ship's main engines powered up.

"We're going right now?"

"Why not? This might be our last chance. We'll make the journey in three or four jumps. That should give us time to stop and assess as we get closer."

"And if the computer's right and there's someone out there?"

"If they're friendly, we start first contact protocols. If they're not..."

Ket grinned. "If they're not then you steer and I'll shoot."

The Vardarian empire was relatively peaceful, but that didn't mean they were pacifists. Their ship, the

Santar, was a royal cruiser equipped with enough firepower to protect itself and its occupants. By approaching in a series of jumps they'd have time to gather information and begin the process of translating any new languages into Vardarian. If this wasn't another false reading, they'd be ready by the time they arrived at their destination.

Please, don't be another false lead.

***

Releasing May, 15th, 2018

Pre-Order it Today

ABOUT THE AUTHOR

Susan lives out on the Canadian west coast surrounded by open water, dear family, and good friends. She's jumped out of perfectly good airplanes on purpose and accidentally swum with sharks on the Great Barrier Reef.

If the world ends, she plans to survive as the spunky, comedic sidekick to the heroes of the new world, because she's too damned short and out of shape to make it on her own for long.

You can find out more about Susan and her books here:
www.susanhayes.ca

www.ingramcontent.com/pod-product-compliance
Lightning Source LLC
Chambersburg PA
CBHW021248200726
48288CB00015B/3038